Church Boyz III

Sins of the Flesh

CHURCH BOYZ III

Sins of the Flesh

www.BeastAuthor.com

ISBN-13: 978-1519778888
ISBN-10: 1519778880

From Darkness to Light

"I have my notes from Calculus class. Did you want to take a look at them?" Gabriel asked. He held his notebook in his hand and waved it like it was a piece of candy. "They're annotated with notes I took during study sessions with the TAs. I'm sure most it will be on the exam coming up next month."

Lamar slowly looked up from his laptop and leveled an evil glare at Gabriel. He looked annoyed. Without saying a word, he cut his eyes, covered his ears with his Beats headphones and shook his head. Lamar went back to ignoring Gabriel and doing whatever is was that he was working on with his laptop.

A heavy sigh of defeat parted Gabriel's lips. Mending fences with Lamar seemed more and more hopeless with each passing day. He had hoped that the time away from each other during Christmas break would have helped to smooth things over. But Lamar was intent on not letting go of his grudge. Gabriel knew it was his fault.

He stared at Lamar. They hadn't spoken to each other in weeks. Things were fine once they'd gotten back to school after Thanksgiving break. Lamar was friendlier. Too friendly. He tried dragging him out to gay clubs and introducing him to discreet gay guys. Gabriel understood that his roommate was trying to help but it was all too much. Then one day, when Gabriel didn't want to go out despite Lamar's persistent encouragement he just exploded.

The conversation was a bit fuzzy now but Gabriel remembered saying that he didn't want to be around a bunch of faggots and he already had a man. He was sure the part that made Lamar upset was when he called his roommate a whore and said something about him fucking Micah. Gabriel could never forget the shock and then anger that crossed Lamar's face. The young collegian hadn't uttered a word in Gabriel's presence since.

Gabriel pulled his gaze from his roommate and tried to focus on his studies. He needed to ace all of his classes this semester. The stakes were much higher this time around. But as much as he wanted to be diligent and get some work done he couldn't. There was way too much going on in his life. And it wasn't just the rift between him and Lamar.

His father hadn't spoken to him, Micah or Isaiah since the day his mother outed him at Thanksgiving dinner. Last December was the first time in his life that he didn't spend Christmas with his family. It wasn't all bad though. Jermaine had flown down and they drove to Miami and stayed all the way through New Years. It was amazing.

But even a vacation with the love of his life couldn't reign in his worry for Micah. His brother, Micah, had been sitting in county jail facing assault with a deadly weapon charges.

Isaiah had put money on his books so he could call them but Micah never did. Thinking about Micah locked up and dealing with seeing Jabari and that dude Keith together made Gabriel worried. He just prayed that his brother wouldn't hurt himself.

Gabriel closed his eyes and rubbed his temples. He had to focus. If he didn't get the grades he would have to drop out of school. His parents had paid for the spring semester but there was no guaranteeing they'd continue funding his education. He needed to get at least a 3.5 GPA to get a scholarship and even then he might need a job.

Staying in that room was unbearable. Gabriel knew he wasn't going to get any work done. He stuffed his work in his book bag and threw on a jacket. He looked back at Lamar, about to tell him he was going to the library but stopped, knowing the boy probably didn't care. Gabriel opened the door to his dorm room and couldn't believe his eyes.

"I was just about to text you," Jermaine said, looking up from his cell phone. "How you doing baby boy?"

Gabriel smiled from ear to ear. He wanted to jump through the door and hug his man. Thinking about kissing him sent chills through his young body. But he knew better. Gabriel didn't forget where he was.

"What are you doing here?" he asked. Excitement danced on his tongue. "I was just on the phone with you this morning. When did you get in?"

"About an hour ago. I was trying to surprise you. Wanted to see the look on your face when you saw me. Priceless." Jermaine frowned playfully. "You going to let me in so I can hug that tight little body and kiss you until my lips are numb?"

Gabriel looked over his shoulder. Jermaine got the hint. They'd discussed the issue with Lamar many times. The last thing Jermaine wanted to do was add more drama to the situation.

"What's up, Jermaine?" Lamar called out. "You coming in or what?"

Jermaine put a grin on his face and stepped inside. "How's it going, Lamar?"

"Can't complain, my dude. Trying to study for all these fucking finals these assholes have coming up back to back next month. I didn't know you were coming to visit."

"Yea," Jermaine said with a shrug, "just flew in not too long ago. Wanted to surprise this little knucklehead. Figured he could use a break from all the stress of college. You know?"

"That's definitely wassup. He's lucky to have you. How long you staying?"

"Well," Jermaine smiled and looked at Gabriel. "I'm actually here to move into an apartment I just got a couple of blocks away."

"Are you serious?" Gabriel asked. "Oh my God! Wait, you're not done with school. You have a whole semester left. Please tell me you're not dropping out."

"I'm not dropping out. I only need six more credits. I took classes every summer so that I'd have time to job hunt my senior year. I'm taking two independent study classes. Only need to check in with my professors every once in a while."

Gabriel frowned. "How can you afford an apartment? I didn't know you were working? And won't all that flying back and forth be expensive?"

"Relax. We'll have all the time in the world to

talk about how it will all work. I was hoping that the place would be ready so I could take you to see it but I can't get in there until tomorrow. Want to come with me and get a room?"

"I want to," Gabriel started. "But I have an eight o'clock class in the morning and I have so much work I need to do it doesn't make any sense."

"I know you're not telling me that you can't make some time for me. I came a long way just to see you." Jermaine smiled. "Don't leave me hanging, baby."

"We can do dinner and hang out. I really have to get this work done before I do anything. You know I have to make the grades this semester."

"Well," Lamar said. "Why don't you stay here? My home girl over at Spelman wanted to study with me. Which really means she wants to have sex. I could stay at her apartment. I'm sure she wouldn't mind. She could get the dick a couple times."

"You sure?" Jermaine asked. "I don't want to put you out your room, man. Especially when you need to be in a comfortable space to study."

"It's all good, dude. Need to get out anyways.

And I'm sure Gabe here wouldn't mind the company. He's been kind of down in the dumps lately."

"I appreciate that, man."

"Yea," Gabriel said. "Thanks."

"Not a problem, Gabe." Lamar gathered his books, laptop and threw some clothes in his book bag. "See you guys in the morning. Just don't leave any sticky surprises in my bed."

Lamar squeezed out the door with a tight lipped smile. Gabriel watched him go, baffled and dumbfounded. Even when the door closed behind his roommate he was still in shock.

"You okay, babe?" Jermaine asked. He wrapped his arms around Gabriel's waist and kissed him on the forehead. "Look like you saw a ghost or something."

"Yea, I'm fine. I just feel like I tripped up into some alternate dimension or something. It's been so long since I heard Lamar speak that I almost forgot what his voice sounded like. He hasn't said a word to me in weeks."

"Well, don't stress it too much. He's gone. I'm here. How about you try to live in the moment?"

Gabriel's confused frown melted from his face

as he turned and looked up at Jermaine. He smiled. As corny as it sounded, he got a warm and fuzzy feeling inside. Being around Jermaine always made him feel better. Gabriel reached up and laced his fingers behind his man's neck. Slowly, he pressed forward and pressed his lips against Jermaine's.

Tasting Jermaine's soft, firm lips put Gabriel on cloud nine. For a moment, all the worries in the world were gone. The only thing on the struggling coed's mind was how good it felt to kiss his boyfriend. Pulling away for a breath of air was the hardest part.

"I missed you," Jermaine said. He looked Gabriel in the eyes. "I missed you so much."

"It's only been a few weeks," Gabriel said with a giggle. "But I missed you, too. Hated thinking about waiting until Spring Break to see you again."

"Yea, I wasn't about to let that happen. I would have come down or flown you up for a weekend or something."

"I know. But what are you doing here? And what's all this about an apartment?"

"Like I said, I leased an apartment right down

the street. You can walk to class and everything."

Gabriel frowned. "What do you mean I can walk to class? You mean I can walk to the apartment whenever I want to, right?"

"No," Jermaine took Gabriel's hands in his own. "I mean I want you to live with me. You'll be there alone most of the time because I'm still taking classes but when I'm here we'll be together. Living together. If you want."

Gabriel smiled. He was happy that Jermaine wanted to be close but it all seemed a lot. Despite being together for nearly six months, Gabriel couldn't help but wonder if moving in together was too much, too soon. They'd spent more time apart than together. Sure, they loved being all up under each other when they saw each other but living in the same space was different. Gabriel figured that out by living with Lamar.

"You don't think it's too soon?" Gabriel asked. "Maybe we should wait until you actually move down here for good."

Jermaine reached up and caressed Gabriel's cheek. He smiled, hiding his disappointment. "Whatever you are comfortable with is fine with me. You'll have a key and you'll always know when I'm there. Cause I'm going to want you there with me. I love you, Gabe."

"I love you, too." Gabriel hugged him and squeezed tight. "Now, how on earth are you able to afford an apartment and all this traveling? You don't have a job, Jermaine."

"You know I'm a Finance major. I've been trading stocks since I was a junior in high school. Cashed in some shares and put some extra money in my pockets. Even got my mom a new car."

"Guess I found me a man with money."

"Please, I made a couple of lucky trades and was blessed. Wanted to put the money to good use and maybe set a foundation for you and me."

"Just give me some time to think about it. Living together is a big step. I've never been in a relationship or been in love, until now. It's all new."

"And I'm not going to rush you. When you make a decision I'll be fine either way. As long as you don't break up with me. That would kill me."

"As long as you're not playing with any of those guys that are trying to get at you back at school we're cool."

"Why would I stray when I have all I need right here?" Jermaine asked. He kissed Gabriel again, savoring the softness of the boy's touch. "You talked to your parents? You haven't said anything about them in a while."

"Nope. Sometimes I wonder if I should call them but I can't do it. Part of me is still mad at my mom. Another part is scared what they'll say. They might disown me. I just keep hoping that they just need some time and space."

"I wish I could tell you the answer, but I honestly don't know. I came out to my mom after my freshman year and she looked at me like I was stupid. Said she knew I liked boys since I was in elementary school. So she already knew. Nothing changed. I was just relieved to not have to lie anymore."

"Too bad my folks aren't that understanding. Maybe it was just that all three of us were gay or bi or whatever. Finding about Isaiah really surprised me."

"Yea."

Gabriel cocked his head to the side. "Did you and Isaiah mess around back in high school? Please don't lie to me, Jermaine."

"Why does it matter?" he blurted out. "Will it change how you feel about me? Will it make a difference?"

"It won't change anything. I just want to know. I don't want to be the only one in the room not knowing what's going on when I'm with the man I love and my brothers."

"Look, it was high school. I messed with Isaiah, Micah and Jabari. We all experimented with each other. The funny part is that Micah had no idea about Isaiah until ya'll little dinner drama."

Gabriel slipped his hand from Jermaine's. He walked over to his bed and flopped down. He knew he couldn't be mad about Jermaine having a history but he had a hard time getting over the fact that his boyfriend had been intimate with both his brothers. He felt as though he was the last prize to be won in some crazy competition.

"Please don't be mad," Jermaine said. "I was a silly teenager. No of that shit matters."

Gabriel looked up at him and said, "Maybe I'm just a silly teenager. Falling in love with a man who's been with my siblings. I'm not mad. But it's a lot."

"I know. Just don't give up on us because of what happened in the past. We both have to look forward." Jermaine kneeled down in front of Gabriel and took his face in his hands. "And you are not a silly anything. You're smart as Hell and charming as fuck. Anyone would be lucking to call you their boyfriend. I just hope that you're not going to make me stop using that word when I talk about you."

Gabriel frowned. "Who are telling I'm your boyfriend?"

"I told my mom. She wants to see you. It's been a while."

"Wow, it has. I don't think I've seen your mom since I was like fourteen."

Jermaine rubbed the back of his neck and said, "Yea, she asks like every time I talk to her how old you are. She can't imagine you as the grown man that you are."

"Oh, now I'm a grown man, hunh?" Gabriel asked, jokingly. "When did that happen?"

Jermaine sat next to him, reached over and cupped the bulge straining against his jeans. "I don't know. You tell me. When did this happen?"

"Been like that since you walked through the

door," Gabriel said with a giggle.

"Yea, yea," Jermaine mocked. He leaned back on his elbows and cocked his head to the side. "So what's going on with Micah? Have you heard from him."

Gabriel shook his head, "No. Isaiah put money on his phone but he aint use it. He even went up to the county jail but Micah refused to see him."

"Your brother has always been the most stubborn dude I know. I just couldn't imagine sitting in someone's jail. That shit is crazy."

"Watching him stab Jabari was some crazy shit. I couldn't believe it when it happened. If Isaiah didn't stop him the boy would be dead."

"I was home last week, when I got my mom the car, and went to church. No one even knows what happened. How is Jabari?"

"I don't really talk to him. But Isaiah said he was up and walking around again. That surgery took a lot out of him. Heard he missed the first couple of weeks of school."

Jermaine sighed and shook his head. "Thank God Micah didn't kill that boy. Murder charges would have been Hell. You think he can beat those assault charges?"

"I don't see how. That dude that came for Jabari will probably testify even if me and Isaiah don't. Plus the police have the weapon and DNA of Jabari's blood all over Micah. It doesn't look good."

"I'm sorry, baby. I know it's a lot to deal with, especially now. Still no word from your parents?"

"Nope. That's why I need to get this work done. If I want to be here next year than I have to get one of those scholarships and maybe a job."

"It will all work out," Jermaine said, hugging him. "I'll always make sure my baby is taken care of, believe that."

Gabriel smiled up at Jermaine. He loved the sentiment behind the gesture but he didn't want to have to really on anyone but himself. More than anything he wanted to be able to take care of himself. Moving in with Jermaine seemed like a fun idea but now he was talking about financially taking care of him. It was a lot and fast.

"I can take care of myself, Jermaine."

Jermaine sucked his teeth, "You sure about that?"

In one smooth, swift move, Jermaine leaned in and planted his lips on Gabriel's. He was slow and gentle. Savoring the soft touch of the boy's lips pressed against his own. Jermaine let himself fully experience the kiss, focusing on how wet and warm Gabriel's flesh felt on his. Slowly, he opened his mouth and dragged his tongue over his man's plump bottom lip.

"You really going to do this now?" Gabriel asked between kisses. "Just going to knock me off my flow."

"I'm a man that lives in the moment." Jermaine pulled at the boy's lip with his teeth until it slipped free. "I've got so much sexual tension pent up I'm going to fucking explode if I can't have you right here, right now. Besides, shouldn't we get it out the way?"

"You know I can play in your ass over and over again without getting anything out of the way."

"Well, I was thinking that you'd let me tap that this time. Aint played in that ass for a good minute."

Gabriel shifted in the bed. He'd only bottom for Jermaine a few times before and it had always been difficult. Jermaine wasn't as large as he was but he wasn't small and his dick was on the long side.

"I don't know if I'm prepared for that right now."

"If you don't want to bottom just say so, Gabe," he said with a frown. "I don't want to pressure you into doing something you don't enjoy or don't want to do."

"I'm just not used to it. I want to give you what you want but it's not easy."

"It's cool. Go ahead and study. I need to take me a nap anyways. Been a long ass day."

Guilt hit Gabriel in the chest as he saw a cloud of disappointment darken Jermaine's face. First he wondered if he was just being selfish. When they had sexy, he usually fucked Jermaine at least three times. But he did like it. Then again, he took it even after he nutted just so Gabriel would be satisfied. Gabriel knew how it feel to have a dick move in side of him after nutting. That was usually the problem. He nut like five seconds after Jermaine got it halfway in and started moving.

He watched Jermaine lie back on the bed and flash a smile up at him. Gabriel felt like shit. The man had flown all the way down, gotten apartment and was promising the world for him and he couldn't at least give him some ass this once. Jermaine loved him and Gabriel loved him back.

"Pull down your pants," Gabriel ordered. "And don't talk."

Excitement poured over Jermaine's face like he was about to feel some pussy for the first time in his life. He thrust his jeans and underwear down to his feet and kicked them down to the ground. His dick feel back to his stomach, making a loud smacking sound. Gabriel wondered if he had bitten off more than he could chew.

Instead of focusing on how much it would hurt, Gabriel thought about how happy he would make Jermaine. He stood up and began to strip. Despite his own insecurities, he took off his clothes slowly and tried to look as sexy as he could. Jermaine had told him over and over again how sexy he was. Gabriel figured it was time he started believing his man.

Naked, Gabriel climbed on the bed and moved between Jermaine's legs. The urge to grab him by the back of his thighs and work on his hole was overwhelming. Gabriel had to remind himself over and over again that tonight was about

Jermaine, not him.

It began with soft, lingering kisses on Jermaine's inner thighs. Gabriel worked his way up until he was eye to eye with the black snake. He flicked his tongue out and dragged it over his man's heavy sack until his dick strain from pleasure.

Gabriel leaned forward, dragging his chest and then abs over Jermaine's brick hard prick. He could feel the slick precum smear his skin. When their dicks pressed together, Gabriel grinded his hips and leaned in for a deep passionate kiss. If he could get Jermaine super horny and make him bus that much faster, all this work was worth it.

Jermaine groaned, reached up and smacked both Gabriel's cheeks with his hands, hard. It caught the boy off guard and threw him off his rhythm for a second. He giggled nervously and went back to kissing and dry humping. Jermaine pried his small ass cheeks apart and exposed his tight, near virgin ass.

"Baby, you got me leaking," Jermaine moaned. "I want to feel that ass on my dick. Stop teasing me."

"I'm just trying to set the mood," Gabriel said,

playfully. "Want you good and ready."

"Shit, I'm ready. What you're doing is being cruel. Let me feel you."

Gabriel forced a smile on his face. He leaned in and kissed Jermaine. At a snail's pace, he went to his neck, kissing inch after inch. Then Gabriel attacked his man's nipples. He'd always loved when he pulled at them when they fucked. He nibbled on them and knew he was doing something right when he felt Jermaine's dick smack up against his stomach.

Gabriel was running out of skin. He ran his tongue over each flexed abs and drew circles with the tip. When he got to the prize, Gabriel didn't cower. He took Jermaine's dick by the base and began to work.

He stroked it slowly, milking the precum from Jermaine's shaft to the tip of his dick. Gabriel ran his tongue over the dick head slit and smeared the natural lubricant all over the head. Then, he took him in his mouth. Sucking the head until it was bulging with blood and straining on his tongue.

Jermaine's hips thrust up and jabbed the back of Gabriel's throat. The boy gagged but forced himself to endure. His throat muscles relaxed and he started sucking. He focused on the head and slowly made his way down. It wasn't until his nose grazed Jermaine's pubes a few times that he realized he was pretty good at giving head.

Gabriel was in a groove. The sound of a condom wrapper tearing open tripped him up. He glanced towards Jermaine and saw him pulling a Magnum from the wrapper. Jermaine sat up, pulling is glistening dick from Gabriel's mouth, and covered his dick. He looked at Gabriel with lust and expectation in his eyes.

Gabriel offered a weak smile. He reached over Jermaine's body and got the bottle of lube he'd typically used for jacking off. There was no way he was going to attempt anything without a gallon of lube at his reach. Gabriel climbed on top of Jermaine, stroking his stiffness with a generous amount of lube.

Jermaine reached up and took hold of Gabriel's hips. "Take your time. I want you to try and enjoy me inside of you. If you want it to be, it can be one of the most amazing experiences you ever have. Trust me."

With a nod, Gabriel focused his mind on the task at hand. He gripped Jermaine's insanely hard dick. It seemed bigger. He rubbed it up and down the crack of his ass until the tip nestled itself against his quivering hole. Gabriel swallowed hard. It was time.

He pushed back slowly. It already hurt. Gabriel ignored the pain. He thought it might just be shadow pain since Jermaine wasn't even inside yet. He rocked back and forth, forcing his hole to accept that a dick was coming in and there was no way to get out of it.

After five minutes of trying, Jermaine's dick head finally popped through Gabriel's tight sphincter. The boy clawed at Jermaine's chest with his other hand and his legs shook like he was already nutting. He swore something had torn. He leaned forward and rub his finger over his aching hole. Still smooth and throbbing.

Gabriel leaned back again. He let Jermaine's dick slide in his hole without complaint. One inch, two inches, three…He paused and took in a couple of deep breaths. His ass felt like it was getting ripped open and there was this uncomfortable feeling in his gut. Still, Gabriel was determined to finish and take care of his man.

"You feel so fucking good," Jermaine whispered. "Take your time. I got you."

Gabriel nodded and inched back some more. His body steeled when he felt Jermaine's dick jump inside of him. He shot the boy a hard stare, warning him not to do it again. Satisfied, Gabriel sat back and bottomed out on Jermaine's dick. He was sweating bullets. He couldn't believe that he'd actually taken the whole thing. He looked down at Jermaine and smiled.

"You do know that sex includes movement?" he teased. "We're not done yet. We're just starting."

Gabriel's eyes glazed over. He tried to focus but that shit wasn't working anymore. All he could think about was how badly he felt like he had to shit and the pinching pain on his anus. Then Jermaine started making his dick jump again. Gabriel slapped him on his chest.

"Why you keep doing that?!" he demanded. "That hurts!"

"I'm trying to get you used to it. Trying to open you up. You won't be able to take me unless you relax and open up. Now, each time you feel my dick jump inside of you, make your dick jump too."

Gabriel nodded. Jermaine's dick jumped and then Gabriel made his jump too. He smiled in surprise when he realized that his hole tightened when he made his dick jump. They did it over and over again until the pain the disappeared. Gabriel made his dick jump and held the muscled tight, squeezing as hard as he could.

"Oww!" Jermaine said, smacking him on the ass. "You little fucker."

Gabriel smiled. "I'm just showing you that I'm a quick study."

"Is that right? You don't mind taking instructions?"

That question made Gabriel nervous. He bit at his bottom lip and looked down at Jermaine. He trusted him. Gabriel knew that Jermaine would be gentle and not try to hurt him. He'd take his time. Gabriel took a deep breath and nodded.

Jermaine sat up and pulled Gabriel tightly against his body, his dick still deep in his boyfriend's gut. In a swift move, he spun the novice bottom on his back. Jermaine leaned down and kissed him. It was a soft kiss meant to give strength. Jermaine peered down into his man's eyes.

"I'm not going to hurt you," he began. "Just push out when I push in. Trust me."

Gabriel looked him, worried at how sound the advice he was given actually was. He didn't have time to argue. Jermaine pulled half the length of his dick from his hot hole. He lingered there for a moment, giving Gabriel a look that could only mean one thing: get ready.

Jermaine drove the length of his sheathed meat deep into Gabriel's gut. The boy pushed out and waited for the pain to come. It didn't. H felt a hard pressure against his prostate. The foreign sensation made his dick jump. He looked up at Jermaine and smiled like he'd discovered gold.

Jermaine's hips moved slowly at first. Gabriel's body got used to the invader. He stopped trying to slow his man's anal assault by blunting him with his legs. Gabriel pointed his behind his head and gave his over without restraint. Jermaine took the message loud and clear.

Soft moans and shuffled grunts hummed in the room. Jermaine sat back on his heels and started long dicking the boy. Trying to hit his prostate. Gabriel's head thrashed back and forth.

He wanted to stroke his dick but he knew he would definitely explode if he did. Jermaine's humping only got faster and harder.

"Baby, you're going to make me nut," Jermaine moaned. "You feel so fucking amazing."

Jermaine reached down and gripped Gabriel's heavy dick in his hand and stroked it in sync with his thrusts. Gabriel came first. His dick stiffened hard as a brick and thick globs of cum squirted at over his chest. His clenching ass sent Jermaine over the edge. He pulled his dick out and flung off the condom. It only took two pumps to release the seed boiling deep in his balls.

Spent, Jermaine, collapsed on top of Gabriel and kissed him. The two lay there in euphoric bliss, basking in the glow of orgasm. The pair didn't even hear the door open. But they definitely heard the clapping.

"Fucking bravo," Lamar said. "That was some fucking performance. For a minute I didn't think you would be able to take his dick, Gabe."

"What the fuck are you doing, Lamar?" Jermaine said. "This shit isn't funny."

"This wasn't a comedy." Lamar put his finger to his chin and feigned an expression of deep thought. "Can't exactly call it a porn. Maybe a very graphic love story about the first time a boy gave himself to a man. You are eighteen, right?"

"Lamar," Gabriel started, "Please just get out."

He held his hands up. "Fine, fine." Lamar walked over to Gabriel's laptop on the desk and logged in. That made Gabriel nervous, that he had his password. He typed a url in the web browser address bar and a live image of them popped on the screen. "Remote recording is fucking amazing. Isn't it?"

Lamar walked out of the room, laughing. Gabriel jumped up and went to the computer. Somehow, Lamar had live broadcasted him having sex with Jermaine with his own laptop. And from the counter on the screen, at least a hundred people had watched. There was no telling how many checked in to see who was online and logged off after seeing Gabriel.

Rage gathered in Gabriel's gut. He stampeded out of the room, naked. He saw Lamar at the end of the hall and sprinted towards the boy. It wasn't until he was an arms length away that Lamar realized what was going on.

Gabriel slammed the heel of his foot in the

small of Lamar's back. The freshman went crashing to the ground, his body twisting in a very unnatural pose. Gabriel was about to jump on his but Jermaine picked him up off his feet and dragged him back. A crowd was forming.

"Fucking faggot!" Lamar screamed. He laughed. "Don't get mad at me because you dick hungry."

"Let that shit go," Jermaine said. "Just come to the apartment tomorrow and you won't have to deal with this shit. If you really want to, we can look at what it would take to transfer to GSU or something."

Gabriel fumed. It wasn't until that moment that he understood how violated his brother Micah had been. Lamar was going to get his. That much, Gabriel was certain of.

Forsaken

"Ay, bruh. They about to serve breakfast." My cellmate tugged on my blanket and woke me up. "You coming to eat or you staying in bed again?"

"I really aint got no appetite to be honest," I replied. I stretched my arms towards the wall. I saw dude's eyes travel down and then quickly back up. I had to stop myself from laughing at the fact that he'd peeped my morning wood. "Why, you want that shit?"

"I mean, if you don't mind." He rubbed his stomach and smiled. "You know a nigga can eat."

I nodded as I pulled the covers from my body. My eyes stayed glued to his as I climbed down from the top bunk. I made sure my dick was in plain sight. Teasing this self-professed pussy killer had been my only entertainment since being locked up at county. The days were long and the nights even longer. Luckily, I was in the cell with a dude that had hygiene and wasn't too rough on the eyes. He just wasn't that smart.

"I got you man, I'll probably just eat the nasty ass biscuit. Don't really like that powdered egg shit or the nasty ass meat they try to pass off as sausage."

"Cool, cool." He went to the door and looked back. I caught him staring at my dick again. "I'll see you out there. And Micah, make sure you sit next to me. I don't want none of them niggas trying to get that shit."

I nodded my understanding and watched his thick ass walk out of the cell. Mario was about six-foot two inches with tats all over his almond complexioned skin and had abs that could break bricks. He had a homely face, kind of like a boy next door type shit. He was attractive enough. Even the chipped front tooth of his was sort of cute. It gave the dude character.

My dick thickened against the prison boxers. I groaned in frustration. It had been so long since I had busted a nut that I forgot what it felt like to fill up a nigga's ass. Seventy-five days and counting. After what all went down with Jabari I just hadn't been in the mood to chase after some ass or even jack off. Sad thing was that there were plenty of undercover dick hungry dudes up in the county with me.

Today was different. I'd be walking out this bitch on a bond by this afternoon. No one knew I was going to bounce, not even my family or my cellmate, Mario. The less anyone knew about what the fuck I had going on the better. I made sure to let my lawyer fuck-buddy know that he wasn't to tell anyone I was getting out. The last thing I needed was to have folks asking how I posted a $50,000 bond. Plus I had moves to make.

I went to the metal commode, leaned over to aim my hard dick and relieved myself. The urge to stroke my dick and bust all over the seat was overwhelming. But it would be a waste. I needed to play in some ass to celebrate my impending fucking freedom. I hated wasting my seed.

Annoyed, I pulled out the blue uniform the guards gave me when I was processed in and got dressed. I took a deep breath before I stepped out into the main floor. Dealing with all the drama these career jail birds riled up was stress I didn't need. The assault charges I was facing were enough to have me damn near a panic attack.

Mario waved me over once I got my tray. Dude wanted to make sure I wasn't going to let anyone get this tray. I went over to him and his little crew and sat down. I tried to drown out the conversation they were having. It was the same conversation every day. Females and how they ran shit on the outside was all they talked about. Something told me to go back to the cell and try to sleep the day away.

"When you getting out this bitch, Micah?" One of the old heads asked. "Your pops is the deacon at a church. I know that nigga got some kind of pull."

"I'm getting out later today," Not really giving a fuck. These dudes didn't know none of my people. "My boy posted my bond this morning. Just waiting to get processed out."

Mario looked at me. "Damn nigga. I aint know you was about to go free. I'm happy for you but shit, got to break in another nigga in that small ass cell."

"Hopefully he can deal with your snoring and farting in your sleep."

The table cut up laughing. Mario only grinned. Maybe I was tripping but it seemed like he was genuinely upset that I was leaving. Breaking in a new cellie was a lot to deal with but it was the shit you went through when you were in county. Niggas came and went. Only the dudes with crazy ass charges sat there for months after months.

The old head asked me what I was going to do when I got out but the rest of them offered up suggestions before I could even answer. Most of them said I should get me some pussy and then hit up a club and get drunk. They got half of my plans right. But before I could have any type of celebration I had to take care of some business and work on getting these fucking charges dropped.

All the plotting and scheming I had dreamed up for weeks clouded my mind so much that I almost didn't notice how Mario was acting. Dude was usually full of jokes and talkative as Hell. Now, he just ate his food like it was his last meal or something. I kind of felt bad.

There was no scenario where I would be okay with sitting my ass in someone's jail. But I did feel like I was abandoning the man. He was a few years older than me but I was kind of the big brother in the relationship. It wasn't my first time in jail but it was his. I tried to show him the ropes as best I could. Shit, we got close. I knew all about his family, kids and how he tried to hustle to provide for his seed.

When our eyes met I offered him a sympathetic look. I even handed him my biscuit before I went back to the cell. It was jail. There wasn't much comfort I could offer the man. I just hoped he didn't come in the cell, crying and moaning. It would be another hour before we would be let out again and I wasn't in the mood to hear a grown ass man complain about some weak shit.

"So you was just going to leave and not tell a nigga?" he asked as soon as he walked in. "You could have at least gave me a heads up in case I wanted to find someone to come in this bitch when you leave."

"I just told you and them other niggas I was leaving."

"You could have told me earlier," Mario said, the hurt clearly evident in his voice. "We been in this bitch together for like two months. You a cool ass dude and I'd fuck with you on the outside. You like my brother."

"Likewise, man. Best thing you can do is get one of these old heads in your cell. They don't talk much and aint trying to be hard. They really just want to be left alone. You don't need to be fucking with no one that has chip on his shoulder."

Mario nodded. "What time you getting out?"

"I'm guessing five or six. They usually don't start processing until the evening shift comes in because folks have until four to post bail. It will be here quick enough but I'm sure the shit will feel like forever."

"So I have to look at you all day and think about you leaving me?"

My face scrunched up in surprise. "You make it sound like I'm your bitch dumping you or some shit."

"Go head with that shit, man. You know what I mean. Like I said, I'm happy for you. I don't know, just got attached or some shit. Maybe this fucking jail is making me soft. I miss my people. Shit, I might miss you."

"Awe, boy. You want a hug?" I asked jokingly.

Mario didn't say anything. He just looked at the ground like he was actually thinking about saying 'yes' to my question. Dude was acting mad funny. I'd seen him check out my dick and ass before but I just figured it was general curiosity. Men like to compare. Now he had me wondering. There was no way I had been so caught up my bullshit and drama that I didn't see the signs of a nigga that wanted to fuck around on the low.

I narrowed my gaze on the man until our eyes locked. Still, he didn't say anything. So I said fuck it and went towards him. I wrapped arms around his solid frame and squeezed as hard as I could. Slowly, he reached up and hugged me back. We stood there, embraced for an uncomfortably long period of time. I had loosened my grip but he didn't do the same. So I decided to take it a step further.

I lean back until we were face to face. I could see the longing and lust in his eyes even though he tried to hide it. I inched my face closer and closer to his. Mario was still as fuck. I was a breath away from his lips and just took the plunge.

My lips pressed against his. I could feel his hard body shiver against mine. Almost like it was his first kiss. It was probably the first time he kissed another dude. I reached up and took his head in my hand as my lips moved with passionate motives.

I sucked on his bottom lip and then dragged my tongue over his front teeth. I could taste the syrup from the flabby ass pancakes they served for breakfast. He moaned in my mouth and only encouraged me to go further. I reached down the front of his pants and grabbed his dick.

"What are you doing?!?" he asked backing away.

"What the fuck you mean?" I stared at him confused. "I thought it was what you wanted me to do."

"Naw man," he waved at me. "I can't get down

with that faggot shit. You need to keep your distance before I have to fuck you up."

I didn't have the patience for words. I rushed the nigga and had my hand wrapped around his neck. He had me by a good twenty pounds in muscle but I was enraged. I really wanted to just fuck him up. That urge to beat a nigga burned in my chest the moment they put me in this bitch. The feeling overwhelmed my need to bust a nut.

"I don't know what the fuck type game you trying to play but I aint got time for that bullshit."

Mario's shock slowly morphed into a grin that spread form cheek to cheek. "That's what the fuck I want. If we going to do this shit you got to be a nigga ready to man handle me."

I could only shake my head and smile back at his twisted ass. Lust flushed his face. The way he looked at me made my dick instantly hard again. I knew what game he wanted to play and had no problem going with the shit.

"Get on your fucking knees nigga," I ordered. "You bout to suck this dick and I don't want to feel no fucking teeth."

Fear and uncertainty quickly covered his face. I

snarled at him. There wasn't going to be no backing out now. We had crossed the point of no fucking return. I pressed down on his shoulder until he was face to face with the bulge in my pants. My dick jumped a few times before I slipped it out. I didn't even give Mario time to think. That would have just fucked everything up.

"Open your mouth," I commanded. He did as he was told. "Now suck on it like a popsicle."

I pulled his mouth down on my dick and pushed as far down his throat as I could. He gagged at first but then started sucking. His lips covered his teeth and he was going to work. My head shot back and my hips poked out, offering as much dick as I could. This nigga's head game was fucking amazing.

It always amazed me how 'straight niggas' gave the best head. Maybe it was because they just tried harder. Maybe it was the shock of turning out a straight boy that made the experience that much more exciting. Either way, the shit was good.

I drove my hips faster and harder into his mouth. Mario kept sucking without pause. He gripped my waist and ate my dick as if would be the key to his freedom. I only pulled out when I felt my orgasm get a little too close. I looked down at my slob covered meat and smiled. My dick was ready. I just hoped Mario was.

"Get up on that bunk and bend the fuck over."

He held his hands up. "Dude, sucking dick is one thing but I can't take a dick in my ass. That's too fucking homo. Just bust while I suck you off."

I slapped him with the back of my hand. "Bitch nigga, you aint got no fucking choice. You started this shit I'm going to fucking finish it. Now bend that ass over and try to enjoy this dick. Trust me when I say it will be the best you ever fucking have."

Mario rubbed his face and looked at me like I was crazy. I didn't flinch. I just balled my fists and waited for what was going to come next. We stared at each other for a moment. It was a nice little stand-off until I reached down and stroked my slick dick. His eyes went wide. Finally, with a reserved sigh, he pulled his pants down. His dick was fucking huge. His ass was even bigger than I thought. When he bent over I thought I'd melt just from looking at his hole.

Mario's ass was round, brown and muscular as fuck. His hole puckered tight and had a few wisps of hair around it. My mouth watered for a taste. I dove in and tongue lashed his hole with all my strength. Dude was tight but I managed to lick the soft inside of his ass with the tip of my tongue. When I heard his moans get so loud I feared someone would hear I knew that ass was ready.

I smacked my heavy meat against his hole and grinded until I saw precum drip like a faucet. I was horny as fuck. I knew I'd probably nut before I even worked halfway in his virgin ass. I didn't care. I just wanted to pop his cherry and flood his hole.

Mario clawed at the thin jail mattress as I pressed the broad tip of my dick against his hole. It tightened and kissed the head of my pole each time I pushed forward. The sensation drove me wild. Blood raced through my veins. I gripped his hips and tried not to drive my dick in to the hilt. It was so fucking tempting to do so.

"Fuck!" Mario yelled. The head of my dick slide in his hole. Velvety soft warmth greeted my meat. "Slow the fuck down nigga! Shit hurts!"

I didn't move. But it felt like his big ass was sucking my dick into it. My eyes were glued on my dick disappearing in his ass inch by wet inch. I bit down on my bottom lip trying not to nut from the sight of his hole clenching at my dick. It was erotic as fuck.

The throb of my heart pounded in my head. I could feel the heavy beat of my heart all the way down to my dick. It pulsed and throbbed like a living muscle with a mind of its own. I reached down and twisted his nipple hard as I spoke into his ear.

"Stroke that thick ass meat while I fuck this fat ass."

Mario groaned. He reached down and gripped his dick, doing as he was told. His ass tightened the moment he touched his flesh. I grinded into his ass as hard as I could and short stroked his ass. I needed to open him up to fuck him how I wanted to fuck him.

I slammed my dick into his ass the moment I felt movement in his hips. The man didn't skip a beat. He threw his ass back like a power bottom and devoured my dick. Tingling sensations teased my dick and ran throughout my body. Sweat coalesced all over my body as I went to work. Sounds of wet flesh and muffled moans entangled with one another, creating an erotic harmony hitting the walls of the small cell.

"Beat that nut out your dick, nigga," I said. I could feel my own orgasm build to the point of collapse. I just wanted to last long enough to feel his orgasm. "Bust that shit."

Mario moaned hard and breathed faster. His tender walls massaged the full length of my manhood and put me right at the tip of the point of pure pleasure. Then Mario slammed his ass back hard and impaled himself on my dick. His ass jumped and clenched my meat he was nutting. I busted right along with him.

I filled his hole, his pulsing ass milked my dick dry. When I pulled out he was so tight not a drop fell. That shit didn't work for me. I plunged my face between his cheeks and sucked my seed and his ass juice from his hole. Then I spun his built ass around and kissed him with the fluids swirling between us. We both tasted the product of our lust.

Slowly, I pulled from his lips and stared right back at him. He was in a daze. I couldn't help but grin at the fact that he'd been so satisfied. His nostrils flared. The grin on his handsome widened into a full on smile. He licked his lips, tasting the cum and ass juice I'd shared with him. His chest heaved as he looked up at me. I knew the look well. He was ready to go again.

"You going to let me fuck you too?" He asked. "You leaving and shit and I want to feel that ass on my dick before you bounce."

"Lie back," I said. "I'm going to give you what you want but on my terms. Nigga, you packing heavy meat and you not about to rip my ass open."

He nodded with cheesy grin. Mario leaned back and stroked his still hard dick, squeezing the drops of cum still in his shaft. He smeared the natural lubricant on his dick until it glistened. I took a deep breath. Taking his dick wasn't going to be easy. Nigga was lucky I was still horny as fuck. I spit in my hand and fingered my hole.

Once I worked a finger in my ass I turned around and gave him an all access view of the prize he was about to get. I heard him whisper some shit about how tight my hole looked. His large hand gripped my ass cheek the moment I eased a second finger into my ass.

"Nigga, now you just teasing me," he groaned. "Sit on this dick and let me feel that ass wrapped around my shit."

I looked back at him and smiled. Taking dick wasn't usually what I was into but I just off of his excitement. The fact that he wanted my ass so badly had my head in another place. I reached back and grabbed his thick, hot shaft. It felt heavy as fuck in my hand. For a moment I doubted I'd be able to take him.

Mario wasn't going to let my ass go anywhere but on his throbbing dick. He gripped my hips with his rough hands and eased my back towards his swollen manhood. I rubbed the engorged tip of his manhood up and down the crevice of my ass, forcing moans of pleasure over his lips. I could feel his impatience building with the way his nails dug into my flesh. He wanted to fuck me stupid like he probably did girl on the outside.

Slowly, I pushed back, forcing his girth inside my ass. My hole squeezed and tightened, trying to accommodate the monster that demanded entry. Mario pulled me down harder and harder. Sweat pearled on my forehead. I had to concentrate hard as fuck to give him the sexual need he wanted fulfilled. Finally, the broad tip of his dick slipped inside my hole.

"Ah fuck," I moaned as I felt the hot, flexing muscle ease into my bowels. "Your did is fucking thick as Hell."

"You can take it nigga. Take your time. Shit feels good ass fuck."

I bit down on my bottom lip and beat my dick as I sat back and took inches of his dick. He stretched me so wide that the pain was unavoidable. I managed to take half his meat. My legs buckled from the familiar sensation that only a thick dick could offer. My walls gripped his shit, feeling every inch of flesh pressing and poking at the hundreds of sensitive nerve endings.

"Fuck, I never thought some nigga's ass could feel this good," he moaned. "You really trying to turn a nigga out."

I grinned. Dude was challenging me. I pushed back until I felt the coarse hairs of his pubes scrub my ass like a brillo pad. I took a deep breath and started riding his massive meat. I ignored the stabbing pain numbing my sphincter and focused on my dick and his moans.

I don't know if it was my ass creaming or his dick precumming but my hole got wet as a fucking rain forest. Mario dick slipped and slid in my bowel with scary ease. It still hurt but it felt so fucking good. I got so in the zone that I didn't realize that I was bouncing on his shit, slamming against his muscular thighs, so hard that it sounded like an audience giving a standing ovation.

"Nigga, you bout to make me bust all up in this ass," he growled. Mario matched my riding and slammed up into my ass each time I came down on his dick. "Tell me you ready for this nut, Micah. Say that shit!"

"Bust in this ass, boy! Give me that nut!"

I could feel Mario's body steel under me. His body became as hard and rigid as his dick. He pulled me down on his insanely stiff shaft and let loose a violent torrent of cum deep in my bowel. I felt his dick jump with each shot of hot cum. My ass felt full and so damn good. I reached up and grabbed the top bunk as I pulled my own nut from my dick.

Mario leaned up and hooked his massive arm around my waist. He watched as my dick spit out three thick globs of cum. My body tingled and shivers went up and down my relieved body. I jumped when Mario pressed his lips against my side. He ran his fleshy tongue up towards my armpit. His eyes met mine. Mario was a demon of lust.

"Lay down with me for a minute," Mario said. He didn't wait for an answer. "I don't want to leave this ass yet."

Mario pulled me down onto his bunk, his still hard dick impaled in my ass. He pulled the rough covers over our sweaty, cum cover flesh and spooned tightly against my back. Having his hot, hard muscles pressed into me felt comforting as fuck. I didn't want to move either.

"We could have been doing this shit for the last two months," he said. "Had I known how good this shit was I would have been slipped up in your bunk whenever lights went out."

"Nigga, if I had tried you when we was put in this bitch, you would have nutted up. You know a nigga now. I don't go running off at the mouth like other motherfuckers."

"You right," he admitted. Mario smacked his teeth and said, "Now you bout to leave. I wish I had connections like you to post a fucking bail."

"What's your bail?"

"Nothing but $25,000. I just need to put up 10%. But my peoples don't have $2,500 just sitting around and I have no way to pay some bails bondmen. A nigga is stuck in this bitch until the DA wants to make some bogus ass deal."

"What would you say if I told you I could bond you out once I'm out this bitch?"

"I'd call you a fucking liar first. And then ask why you would do that for a nigga you barely fucking know. What you get out of the deal?"

"Besides a second shot at that thick ass?" I asked, jokingly. "But real talk, I got some moves to make and I'm sure I could use a nigga like you."

"I mean, I do my shit but I don't kill niggas or nothing like that."

"Let me worry about the details. I aint going to have you doing no shit that would land you back in this bitch. Plus I can put you on with my lawyer. Nigga is fire as shit."

"Bet. I aint going to turn down the offer to go free. Just don't sit here and have me hoping only to leave a nigga behind. False hope is the worst thing in this bitch."

"I got you," I promised. "We going to be out this bitch."

Mario fucked me again before we were let out. I fucked him a second time when we were put back in the cell after lunch. Nigga had an appetite for sex that paralleled my own. When the guards came for me to leave, he gave me a look that sent shiver up my spine and my dick thicken and ass twitch. I was definitely going to spring his ass. Having a dedicated dude would be priceless with what I was planning.

"You right on time, man," I said as I walked up to Cedric, my lawyer. His 35 year-old ass always looked damn good in a suit. "Been itching to get out that bitch all fucking day."

"I would have had you out weeks ago if you'd called me sooner," he said with a grin. "You know you didn't have to sit up in here. I'm pretty sure I can get the DA to plead you out with a lesser charge and maybe get a year probation."

"Naw, I'm not pleaded to shit. I'm going to get those charges dropped."

Cedric frowned. "Micah, I read the police report and all the statements. The best you can do is cite your mental state. As long as the victim testifies against you, there's no way the charges are going to get dropped. Hell, the DA could press forward without him if they wanted."

"You know I have connections," I said with a grin. "You going to let me stay with you while I'm out? Can't go back to my folk's house."

"You know I don't mind," he said. A devilish smile creased his face. "You going to let me get that dick when I want it?"

"The dick is yours." We walked up to his BMW. "Toss me the keys."

The man didn't flinch. He tossed me the keys. Cedric was smart as fuck and damn good lawyer. His head game was on point and his ass was good as fuck. He could take dick like a pro. Once I fucked him for three hours straight, busting all kinds of nutts in his ass.

Once I hit the highway he was slurping my dick like a corner whore. I knew he could taste and smell the ass on my meat. I was sure that it only riled up his hormones even more. I shot a thick load down his throat as I pressed the gas pedal, pushing one-hundred miles an hour.

I explained that I needed a friend bailed out.

Cedric didn't ask any question. He made a phone call and the money was sent. Mario would be out by the morning and I'd be right there to pick him up in one of Cedric's other cars. Maybe the Porsche.

I fished out my phone from the manila folder the guards had placed my shit in during processing. I hooked it up to the car charger and dialed my baby brother, Gabriel as soon as it came on. I needed to know what was going on with Jabari. I didn't want anyone to know I was out but hoped that his little ass could keep a secret.

"Gabe," I yelled into the phone. "What the fuck you doing?"

"Micah? You out of prison? How long you been out."

"It was county, not prison. I just got out. What's wrong with you? You sound upset. What the fuck did Jermaine do? I'll beat his big ass if you want me to."

"He didn't do anything. He's actually moving to Atlanta and getting an apartment. Surprised me and everything."

"Then why the fuck you sound so damn sad?"

"Lamar busted in the dorm room when I was having sex with Jermaine. Some of the guys from the building had their phones and recorded us. Everyone on campus knows I'm gay. I haven't been to class in days. I've been sitting in Jermaine's apartment."

"I'm going to take care of his ass. You get up and go to class nigga, you need that fucking degree. You too smart not to finish what you started. I'm going to hit you up later. I need you to ask around about Jabari."

"What are you going to do, Micah? You just got out of prison or jail or whatever. I need my brother. You can't be locked up for years."

"Don't worry little, brother. I got you. I'm going to take care of everything."

I hung up the phone before Micah could whine and complain anymore. Lamar was a piece of fucking work. Something told me that he was a jaded fag in disguise. But I had something for his ass. I called up my friend at UNC. Dude was a computer engineer with a big dick and some of the sweetest as I ever had. He was kind of nerdy but the shit kind of turned me on. The thick ass glasses he wore got me hooked on him in the first place.

"Johnnie, I need you to do me a big favor. I'm going to send you a video that I need you to email to every student and faculty member at Morehouse. Then I need you to hack into someone's computer and get some video. And there's a blog I need you to get registration information from."

"You do know midterms are coming up?" he said in his high, squeaky voice. "How am I going to have time to do all that and study?"

"Make time. I'll swing by the dorm later tonight to help."

There was a pause on the other end of the line. "Fine. Hit me when you're on the way. I'll send the video because it will only take a minute but the other stuff I won't do until I see you."

"Fine. I'll call you later."

I pulled up the video I made of Lamar taking my dick the second time we fucked the morning before we left. If dude thought he was going to embarrass my baby brother he had another thing coming. I figured it would probably be a good idea to pay the boy a visit too. Having Mario by side might prove to be beneficial. I turned to

Cedric.

"How you feel about a quick road trip to Atlanta tomorrow?"

Cedric licked his lips. "You going to let me drive?"

"Hell yea, we going to do what we did last time. You ride my dick while you push the whip."

He smiled. I sighed in relief. I didn't want to stretch Cedric's generosity but I needed to take care of some shit. I knew I would have to dick him down one good time and leave him knocked out and exhausted from the dick before I took the car to see Johnnie.

I gripped the wheel and sped towards Cedric's McMansion. Lamar was going to pay for what he did to my blood and Jabari was about to have his little secrets spilled for the world to see. If that nigga didn't do what I said, there would be Hell to pay.

Confession

Isaiah pushed through his apartment door and slammed his suitcase onto the ground. His fists balled, ready to punch into a wall. He was so mad that he wanted to scream and hit something. Releasing the rage that burned inside his heaving chest was the only option. Isaiah huffed and puffed, pulled his arm back and stared at the wall in front of him.

"What are you doing, Isaiah?" Tasha asked. The concern in her voice matched her worried expression. "Something happen down at the church?"

Isaiah shook his head. "I do everything right. And still I lose everything because of Micah's ass. I'm going to strangle that boy if he ever gets out of jail."

"What could Micah have done to you from jail? He's a little criminal but your brother doesn't have connections like the mob. He can't make things happen while he's locked up. Plus, why would he want to hurt you? You two are blood."

"That shit with Jabari finally came back and bit me in the ass," Isaiah explained. "The reverend said the congregation was beginning to ask more and more questions about what Micah did to his son. Supposedly, a lot of them didn't like the idea of the brother of the man accused of assaulting the reverend's son working as choir director. I'm on administrative leave for some shit that I didn't do."

"Alright," Tasha said. She walked up to him and stroked his arm. "How long are you on leave? Everything should die down after the trial in a couple of weeks. I'm sure it will be fine."

Isaiah let out an exacerbated sigh and walked towards the kitchen. "No it won't. You uncle told me that it might be a good idea if I started looking for another job. I have two more paychecks coming but that's it. I'm sure he only offered that because of you."

"You want me to talk to him? It doesn't make since to make you suffer when you didn't do anything."

"True. But I didn't exactly stop him when he was about to carve the reverend's son up like a fillet of fish either. Your uncle is mad at me, too. Probably mad at the whole family. He told me to send his best to my parents. That means he hasn't seen them in a while and doesn't plan on seeing them. Micah screwed things up for the whole family."

"Baby, I know you're stressed out about all this and probably a little scared about what tomorrow will bring. I get it. But we've saved a lot of money and we'll be fine. We've never lived paycheck to paycheck."

Isaiah shook his head. "That money was for the wedding and the down payment on our first house. I don't want to touch that without good reason."

"It's just money. I don't want you finding

some job you hate just to make more money. Maybe this is a sign that you should teach music like you always wanted. I know this woman whose husband is an assistant director at a performing arts school. You can put on productions and write your own music for plays and musicals like you always wanted."

"God, woman, I love you so much." Isaiah looked up at his fiancé and let the stress drain from his face. "What would I do without you? Whenever I doubt myself you are there to remind me why I can't give up. You always know exactly what I need even when I don't."

"I'm your woman and you're my man," Tasha said. She walked over to him and laced her fingers behind his neck. "It's my job to make sure you get exactly what you need whenever you need it."

Isaiah grinned as he watched his fiancé's body language switch from that of a comforting partner to a horny lover. The woman's versatility turned him on more than she could imagine. He wrapped his arms around her slim waist and slowly slid his hands down, grabbing her plump, curvy ass. He picked her up in his arms and pulled her in for a kiss.

"Damn, you taste good," Tasha cooed. She grinded her thick, thigh on Isaiah's lengthening manhood. "You need to come home mad more often."

"The anger didn't do that. You did with your sexy, supportive ass. Been a couple days since we consummated our love."

Tasha playfully slapped Isaiah's chest. "Damn heathen. Nothing gets 'consummated' until rings and vows are exchanged. Don't play with me like that."

"Well, I guess I'm a heathen, fornicator and plain old sinner. Cause it's about to get biblical up in this place, married or not." Isaiah leaned down and sucked in Tasha's scent from her neck. "You going to let me taste that special place?"

Tasha pulled away with a wry grin on her face. She bit at her bottom lip and looked towards the bedroom door at the end of the hall. Isaiah frowned when his woman looked back at him. She was up to something. Tasha looked like the fat kid that ate all the cake and lied about it even though the chocolate was all over his face.

"What's going on Tasha," Isaiah asked impatiently. He looked over her shoulder at the bedroom door. "Who you got up in my bed? I'm not playing."

"Don't sit here and get an attitude. As much as I've been open to letting you explore your sexual desires without judgment, I know you're not about to get mad at me."

Isaiah narrowed his gaze and asked, "Is it a man or a woman?"

"Does it really matter? I like both, just like you. Why should I limit myself?"

Tasha began to strip before Isaiah could utter a single word. Jabari had warned him about what having an open relationship with his cousin would mean. Isaiah had tried to get used to the idea of Tasha dealing with someone else, even if it was another man. But he never imagined that she'd be so reckless and bring the man back to the apartment.

"Are you coming?" Tasha asked.

Isaiah clenched his jaw and followed behind his nude fiancé. Seeing her onion shaped, smooth ass would have had him on brick but the uncertainty of what lay behind the closed door had him too shaken to enjoy the sight. She looked back at him with a seductive gaze and then slowly pushed open the door. Isaiah was awe struck by what he saw.

Two men and two women casually lay in the bed, all butt naked. The women were drop dead gorgeous and the men were fine as fuck. Isaiah's eyes bulged from his head. He was so turned on by the sight before him that the sensory overload could have made him bust on the spot. Not only did they look good, they reeked of eroticism.

"You've been down since all that stuff happened at you're parent's during Thanksgiving. A couple of weeks ago I figured you'd feel better by doing something new and exciting. I got you a gift. Well, two gifts, the other two are mine."

"You got me two men to play with? How much did it cost?"

"Don't worry about that. You know I got money baby. And you'd be surprised at the discount I got once I showed the boys your picture. And don't worry. I got them all tested. Enjoy."

Tasha walked over to the bed and took the two feminine beauties by the hand and led them to the cushy couch in the corner of the room. Isaiah watched at the light skinned woman with the dragon tattoo on her back sat Tasha down, pushed her legs up and devoured her pussy. The other woman was chocolate. Isaiah wondered what she tasted like. She hovered over the first woman and pressed her plump titties into Tasha's face. A hard, heavy hand on Isaiah's shoulder pulled him from the spectacle taking place only a few feet away from him.

"I'm Rico," the somewhat thin, tatted up dude said. "My homeboy, Rock and me are here to do whatever you want. You just need to ask."

Isaiah looked the slim thug up and down. His eyes lingered on the thick, heavy meat dangling between his legs. The boy was blessed with more than good looks. Isaiah looked back at his face and smiled. He was at a loss for words.

"Stop making the man nervous," Rock, the other escort said as he climbed his thick, muscular ass off the bed. "How about we just explore and see what you like. Try to relax and enjoy. Your girl got us for two hours. Aint no rush."

Isaiah nodded and smiled. His eyes traveled over Rock's smooth, hard brown sugar toned skin. He wasn't packing as much meat as Rico but when he took Isaiah by the hand and led him to the bed, Isaiah saw that his large assets lied elsewhere. His butt cheeks were so round and firm that Isaiah was sure the man could bounce a quarter off of them.

"I'm going to take your clothes off," Rico said in a deep husky voice. "If I do anything to make you feel uncomfortable just say 'hold on' and I'll stop. I want you to enjoy every moment and remember this night for the rest of your life."

Rico stepped a breath away from Isaiah's face and began to unbutton his dress shirt. Rock stood behind the suspended choir director, reached around and unfastened his belt and pant button. Isaiah closed his eyes and let himself experience the pure bliss surging through his tired body. The men know exactly how to touch and caress all the right spots.

Waves of pleasure shot through Isaiah's body as Rico leaned in and ran his wet, fleshy tongue over his neck. Rico traced small circles on Isaiah's collar bone as he reached up and grabbed Isaiah's head. The thuggish escort pulled back, looked in Isaiah's eyes and pressed forward. His soft, hot lips connected with Isaiah's like two cars colliding. The boy was rough but sensual at the same time. He poked his tongue between Isaiah's lips as his free hand ran under Isaiah's tank top and over his flexed stomach.

Rock managed to work Isaiah's pants and underwear down to the ground. With measured focus, the buff escort stroked Isaiah's hardening manhood in his meaty hand while he kissed the spot where Isaiah's back began to curve into his ass. His lips sent jolts of pleasure tumbling up and down Isaiah's back.

His ass arched up towards Rock's face and the sex servant took the bait, line and hook. Rock pressed his face between Isaiah's cheeks and nibbled on Isaiah's mounds. An illicit moan shook Isaiah. His body quivered against Rico's flexed flesh. He bit down on the boy's bottom lip, hard.

Mind numbing pleasure ravished the son of a deacon. Isaiah was someone between bliss and purgatory. It was torture how good what was happening to his physical being but he didn't want it to end. He craved more. Isaiah needed more.

Rico pulled back from the lip lock and looked Isaiah in the eyes. His lips curled in an erotic, suggestive smile. Sinful intent flared in his haunting gaze. The look frightened Isaiah just a little. Thinking about all the joys the boy's body could offer made Isaiah's spirit scream out in desire.

"I'm going to suck you dick," Rico said. It was more a statement than a question. "You can be as rough or gentle as you like. I just want to taste you."

Words didn't come. Isaiah bit at his lip and simply nodded. He watched the sex professional ease down to his knees. Rico ran his tongue from the base of Isaiah's rigid pole to the tip. He swirled his tongue over the crown of Isaiah's engorged dick head before he took the meat in his mouth. Isaiah reached down and gripped the man by the shoulders to steady himself.

"Damn, that feels good," Isaiah said. He looked over at Tasha, still getting tongue down by the pair of beauties she'd selected. He smiled at his woman. Isaiah mouthed, "Baby, I love you."

Working in tandem, Rock's tongue plunged as deeply into Isaiah's bowels as it could the moment Rico deep throated Isaiah's thick shaft. Every muscle in Isaiah's body tensed and strained from the over stimulation. Orgasm was fast approaching. Isaiah clenched his eyes shut and let go.

Rico didn't flinch when the first shot of cum hit his tongue. He just sucked harder and faster. Rock pried Isaiah's clenched cheeks and forced his tongue through the man's sphincter spasms. A wave of relief and pleasure washed over Isaiah's body.

Rico stood up, his mouth full of Isaiah's seed, and kissed Isaiah sloppily. Cum and spit swirled between their mouths. Isaiah's dick hardened from the surge of blood racing from his heart, through his veins. He was ready to bust another nutt.

Rock climbed on the edge of the bed and bent over. Rico maneuvered Isaiah behind the bubble butt body builder and smacked him on the ass. The message was clear. Isaiah ran his hands over Rock's large, smooth ass cheeks. When Rock pressed his shoulder flat on the bed, Isaiah saw the most beautiful thing he'd ever laid eyes upon.

Either lube or spit made Rock's puckered hole glisten in the dimly lit room. It was so smooth and looked tight as fuck. Isaiah inched closer, his dick pressing against the man's muscular thigh.

"That nigga ass will have you hooked like it's fucking crack," Rico said. "Go ahead and touch it. Just be careful. Once you get a taste you won't be able to stop."

Isaiah smiled as he reached out and ran his middle finger over Rock's hole. It was slick, smooth and burning hot. Erotic heat radiated from the man's body but his hole was on a whole other level. Isaiah pressed his finger against Rock's entrance and the man's ass just swallowed the digit.

Rock's wet, firm walls caressed Isaiah's fingers. The buff bottom looked back and said, "You going to put in something longer and thicker?"

Isaiah's nostrils flared. He pulled his finger away and gripped his dick. He smacked his heavy meat against Rock's exposed hole. The sound of flesh smacking only made Isaiah's dick harden even more. Even the moans coming from Tasha and her girl sent waves of arousal crashing against his body.

He couldn't hold back any longer. Isaiah lined his dick up with Rock's hole and slowly eased his manhood deep into the man's bowels. He looked down and watched inch after inch disappear. Rock's anal ring gripped and pulsed in rhythm with his thumping heart. It was the most erotic thing Isaiah had seen in a long time.

Rico eased behind Isaiah and whispered, "Fuck his ass good. He won't be satisfied unless you dick him down like slut. He can take everything you throw at him."

Isaiah took the words to heart. He pushed down on Rock's back and pounded away at the man's ass like there was no tomorrow. Rock took each violent stroke like a pro. He threw his ass back, meeting Isaiah's hips in mid thrust each time. Their bodies collided in animalistic pleasure. It was an abomination how raunchy they fucked.

Every nerve ending in Isaiah's brick hard dick tingled from the sensations Rock's insides offered. If he hadn't know any better, Isaiah would have sworn he was lost in the rapture, digging deep inside of Rock's guts.

Rico came behind Isaiah and said, "I can make this shit ten times hotter if you let me."

Isaiah nodded without thought. Rico ran his hands up and down Isaiah's sweat slickened back until he settled at the crack of the man's ass. Isaiah felt something slick and wet ooze between the crack of his ass. He was sure it was lube. Then he felt Rico's dick grind between his ass cheeks.

Isaiah's legs almost buckled the moment he felt Rico's incredibly thick dick rub against his hole. He slowed his anal assault on Rock and let Rico work his magic. Thinking about what it might feel like to fuck and get fucked at the same time put a lusty grin on Isaiah's face.

"I want you to relax and open up for me," Rico said. He voice was so damn smooth and sexy. "I'm going to go slow. I don't want to hurt you."

Isaiah pressed his hips forward, driving his dick in Rock's ass to the hilt. He arched his back and poked his ass out, giving Rico better access to his wanting hole. Isaiah's nails dug into Rock's shoulder when he felt the pressure build from Rico's dick against his entrance. A pain laced moan of pleasure screeched from his mouth once the head plopped inside.

"Squeeze that ass on my dick," Rico ordered. Isaiah followed instructions. Making his dick jump and hole tighten. Rock even moaned a little under him, feeling his dick thicken. "There you go. Just like that. Now fuck that nigga and throw that ass back on this dick."

Isaiah pulled out a little, backing into Rico's dick until it hurt too much to go any further and then pushed back inside Rock. He did the motion over and over again until he felt Rico's low hanging balls slap against his own. Having his prostate jabbed with a thick dick while fucking another man in the ass was purely amazing.

It wasn't long before Isaiah's strokes became more elaborate; faster and longer. He pounded Rock's ass and submitted his hole to Rico's dick at the same time. He closed his eyes and got lost in the sauce.

The three men moaned and groaned. Their bodies tangled like an erotic work of art. Sounds of lust fueled passion bounced violently against the walls. Smells of sex danced in the air, intoxicating everyone in the vicinity. It was an orgy of eroticism and sin.

Rock came first. His massive ass shook like his body had been taken over by an earthquake. Rico shot his load deep in Isaiah's bowels shortly after. It wasn't until Isaiah felt the hot seed of the ultra masculine man in his gut that he felt his own orgasm come.

"Oh my God," Isaiah screamed. He pulled his dick from Rock's ass and jacked until nutt exploded from his dick. "I'm cumming!"

Ropes of thick cum splattered all over Rock's ass and hole. Isaiah's body jerked and twitched with each spasm. He collapsed on the man's back, out of breath. He looked over at Tasha. She had a satisfied grin on her face.

"You still have more than an hour left," Rico said. "You can play in this ass if you want."

Isaiah looked at the boy, chest heaving to catch breath, and smile. "Come take a shower with me. I feel dirty. You can wash this sweat and cum from my body."

Rico headed to the restroom, looking over his shoulder the whole way. Isaiah's dick flopped from thigh to thigh, dripping and still semi erect, as he watched the boys small but perky ass sway in the air.

Hot water crashed against Isaiah's back. He looked at Rico, lust burning in his eyes, and motioned for the boy to bend over. There was no going easy or adjustment phase. He buried his dick, balls deep, and fucked the boy until he filled his guts with his third nut of the day. His ass was just as good if not better than Rock's.

Once they finished washing up, Rico asked, "How often do you and your girl do shit like this? I've been doing this for a while and never had something like this happen. Two niggas for the dude and two broads for the female. Ya'll some freaks."

"My girl is everything," Isaiah said with a smile. "She goes beyond the call to make sure I'm satisfied. I love her. She loves me. We do what needs to be done so we get what we want."

"I respect that. Hopefully I'll find me a female as open and willing as yours."

Isaiah frowned. "You not gay?"

"Naw," Rico said shaking his head. "I guess you could say bisexual but I like pussy more than anything. Long as whoever I'm with is pleased I'm good."

"That's wassup, cause trust me, I'm very pleased."

"Baby," Tasha called. She poked her head in the bathroom. "You need to come see this."

Isaiah saw the concern on her face and quickly

grabbed his towel. He was on her heels by the time she scooped up the iPad. He saw the website headline before his girl could utter a word. His eyes went wide with disbelief. Someone was airing out the church's dirty laundry.

"Scandal in NC Mega Church?" Tasha asked. The worried looked lingered on her soft face. "They have to be talking about our church."

"There are half a dozen mega churches in North Carolina," Isaiah offered. He took the iPad and began reading the article. "You're right, they are talking about our church."

Isaiah sat down and read the article again. Someone was publishing a tell all book called Sins of the Flesh that was going to expose all the sexually deviant behavior of the congregation and leaders in the church. Little tidbits had been feed to gossip blogs to get some publicity. No names were mentioned but the line about the engaged choir director picking up men at sports bars sent a chill up Isaiah's spine.

"Baby, I'm not mad. I'm not even going to question you about the bar thing but pictures?"

Isaiah frowned. He looked back at the iPad and scrolled to the bottom of the article. A picture came up. The face was blurred out and so were the two penises in the shot. There was no discernible attribute but Isaiah knew it was him. The other person in the picture had to be Kareem.

"That's me," Isaiah explained. "It was the night before Thanksgiving. I couldn't sleep. I got up and went to go see Jabari. He wasn't in the mood to fool around so we went to a bar. Your cousin introduced me to this kid from the church, Kareem."

"Wait, you mean Deacon Jone's stepson?" Tasha asked. "Are you fucking serious? He's the one that took that picture?" She shook her head and started pacing. "I knew that little fucker was trouble when he got all friendly with my uncle. He's the one writing that book, watch. Kareem has been with you, Jabari and God knows who else. I wouldn't be surprised if he was fucking his step daddy. And he knows everything about the reverend. This is going to be a mess."

Isaiah stood there, staring back at his fiancé, not knowing what to say. He had stepped out on her without permission and now his business was all over the Internet. Isaiah would be the one exposed but both of them would be embarrassed. Their proclivities would be available for public consumption.

Pangs of guilt and remorse shook Isaiah. Because of his libido, he and Tasha's lives would forever be changed. Once the pictures came out and names were dropped, it was over. He couldn't help but obsess over how revelation of his dark sexual desires would affect his job prospects and his ability to provide for Tasha. He questioned whether or not they'd still be able to afford a house. In his mind, the world was over.

"Calm down, Isaiah," Tasha said. She walked up to him and gripped his hands in hers. "I know that mind of yours is racing a million miles a minute. We'll face this like we face everything; together. Now, sit down and think. What can we do?"

Isaiah eased down to the couch and shrugged. "I don't know. That night first and only time I dealt with Kareem. Something told me not to do it but Jabari pretty much gave me the green light saying he could be trusted."

"I'm going to call my cousin," Tasha said. "I know he saw this shit. See what he says."

Isaiah nodded as he watched his girl hurry off back into the bedroom. They were a pair of chickens running around with their heads chopped off. There was nothing they could do. The book was going to drop. The site didn't mention a release date but if they were leaking information and pictures it had to be soon.

Tasha came rushing back in the living room with her phone glued to her ear. She was having a very animated and lively conversation with Jabari. She tossed Isaiah his phone and went back to the bedroom. She was still clearing out the escorts.

Isaiah looked down at his phone and saw that he had four missed calls from a number he didn't know. He groaned on the inside. If someone had somehow figured out it was him in the pictures leaked online than he'd likely get more and more calls. It was starting. Reluctantly, he tapped the number and called it back.

"Nigga, if you wasn't my brother I'd have been fucking you," Micah said, laughing over the phone. "Didn't know you had a body and meat."

"Micah? Where are you calling me from? You got out of jail?"

"It's just a burner so don't save the number.

I'm on my way back to Charlotte. Had to stop by and see our baby brother right quick and make sure everything was good with him. Seems you've been busy. Who's the nigga that took the picture?"

"Why? Does it really matter now? You read the article. It's not just about me. The book is going to put everyone on blast. The church is going to fall."

"Why the fuck do you care? Some chick on Twitter said you were suspended because of me and Jabari fighting. I'm pretty sure that after folks figure out that's you in that picture you won't be in anyone's church."

"It's your fucking fault. Had to go all crazy because Jabari was with that dude. What the fuck is wrong with you? They're going to put you in prison, you know that, right?"

"I'm not going to prison, bitch. I'm going to take care of Jabari's ass just like I took care of that little fucker that was playing games with our little brother. These niggas think shit is sweet cause a dude was raised in a church."

"Wait, what happened with Gabriel?"

"Aside from him moving into an apartment

with Jermaine to play gay house? Why don't you call him and fucking find out? You should have been calling that boy every day since what happened at Thanksgiving. Folks still not talking to him."

"They're not talking to me either, Micah."

"Then fuck 'em. But we need to look out for each other. I pulled some strings and got some money to pay for Gabriel's school next semester in case he doesn't get that scholarship he's working on. But he's going to need help getting books and shit. You need to call him and see how you can help."

"Alright, Micah. Are you done?"

"No. I'm still waiting on you to tell me who took that picture of you."

Isaiah groaned and rubbed his forehead. "Kareem Jones."

A moment of silence passed and then Micah said, "Guess I'll be making a visit to UNC. Ya'll got me jumping from college to college like a nigga on tour. You and Gabe are lucking ya'll blood."

"Don't go messing with that boy," Isaiah warned. "You might be out on bond or whatever but you still facing assault charges. You don't need to catch another case doing something stupid. Not like you can stop the book from dropping anyways."

"Let me worry about what the fuck I'm doing. I got this. You need to learn how to keep your dick in your pants. If you needed to find some discreet dudes to play with you should have came to me. I wouldn't have let you fuck with Kareem's faggot ass."

"Fine. I'm not going to argue with you, Micah."

"Good. I'll hit you up after I make some moves. Go console your fiancé. Tell her I'm going to make all this shit go away. I promise."

Micah hung up before Isaiah could say another word. The eldest brother shook his head. Micah was only going to make things worse like always. He didn't even care how Micah knew Kareem. He just wished Micah left the boy alone. Isaiah watch as the escorts herded from the apartment. He went to the bedroom and saw Tasha sitting down shaking her head.

"Baby, what's wrong?"

"Jabari said that the school is holding a hearing

tomorrow to see whether or not to expel him."

"Why? He didn't do anything? There was nothing in the article that point to him anyways."

"I know, but something else popped up. Some video of him working at Discreet Encounters found its way to one of the Deans. His face is covered but whoever sent the video said it was him. And there was a link to a blog that Jabari has."

"What's on the blog?"

"His dumb ass kept an online diary describing every single sexual encounter he's had in the last four years. He doesn't say anyone's name but from what I've read so far, it's not hard to figure out who he's talking about. I know he had sex with Kareem and Kareem's step father the same night."

Tasha handed Isaiah the iPad. He scrolled through the blog and skimmed some of the entries. It wasn't hard to figure out who the church folks that he messed with were. Some surprised Isaiah and others seemed like obvious guys Isaiah would mess with.

Kareem wasn't the one that leaked this information to Jabari's college. That move was personal. It had Micah written all over it. Isaiah pulled out his phone and called Gabriel. He needed to find out what his brother had done down in Atlanta. Micah was on a warpath. Isaiah just hoped that his brother didn't bite off more than he could chew.

Salvation

I turned off my cell phone and tossed it over on the bed. Nearly a dozen people from my father's church had called asking me whether or not the book that was coming out was about our church. I lied and said it wasn't. I got so tired of lying that I nearly told one of the elder church ladies that it was in fact our church and that my father was having an affair with a married woman.

So much was happening at one time. I shot to my feet and began pacing back and forth in my bedroom. My cousin, Tasha, and I had talked on the phone for nearly an hour. She pretty much confirmed that it was Kareem's little ass that was behind the book. I tried calling the little fucker but it kept going straight to voicemail. If I saw his ass I was going to fuck him up.

First my blog was hacked, video of me fucking at Discreet Encounters were sent to the Dean of Students at my school and then the book. My world was crumbling right the fuck in front of me. Kareem was behind all of it. I felt powerless.

With only one semester left I was about to get expelled from the University of Richmond. For years I'd been careful. We wore masks at Discreet Encounters. I could always deny that it was me in the video. It wasn't like I had any tattoos. And I doubted the disciplinary board would make me strip naked to compare my body to the one in the video. But there was no telling what other evidence Kareem had sent to the dean. I was fucked.

I went over to my laptop and checked my email. I had sent Dean Muller an email over an hour ago requesting a meeting. I needed to find out how serious this hearing tomorrow really was so I could prepare myself for the worst. The thought of having to transfer schools was dizzying. There was no way I could transfer all my credits and graduate on time.

Finally, he messaged me back. I threw on some clothes and was out the door in a flash. My apartment was only about ten minutes from campus. I got there in five. I damn near sprinted to the man's office. I needed answers and I needed them now.

I walked up to the receptionist and said, "I'm here to see Dean Muller. He said he could squeeze me in."

"Your name?"

"Jabari Carlyle. He just emailed me saying that I could stop by to see him."

The woman pulled up something on her computer. It seemed like an eternity passed before she said, "You can go right on in, Mr. Carlyle. The dean is expecting you."

I gave the woman a quick nod and circled her desk. Stopping myself from running to the man's door was difficult as Hell. I put my knuckles to the door, knocking tentatively, trying not to bang. The man called out something I didn't quite hear so I just pushed open the door.

"What the fuck are you doing here," I blurted out. I couldn't believe my eyes. "You're supposed to be in jail. And you're not supposed to be anywhere near me."

Micah stood up, clasping his hands in a nonthreatening manner. "I was just catching up with Malcolm here. I haven't seen him in a few weeks. Wanted to give him an update on where I was with my online classes and see what he's been up to."

"Malcolm?"

"I'm sorry," Micah said with a coy grin. He pointed back at the dean and said, "Dean Muller. He and I go way back. Before I had my little episode and took a leave of absence he and I were pretty tight. He's the one that made sure I took classes so I could come back and finish school."

I looked towards the dean and said, "Sir, why is he here? I thought I was coming in to discuss the hearing tomorrow."

"Son," the dean began. It was odd hearing him say that word since he was barely in his mid-thirties. "Micah is here to facilitate a resolution to our little dilemma. He's come up with a way for us to forego the hearing and avoid the risk of expulsion."

I looked back at Micah. "What do you want, Micah?"

"Just to tip the scales back into balance. You probably think Kareem was the one that sent the dean the video and link to your blog. He wasn't. But once we are done here we have to head back to Chapel Hill to deal with his ass."

I nodded slowly, trying to follow what Micah was saying. I was still taken aback by his close relationship with Dean Muller. I'd never really had any dealings with the man until now. But the more I thought about it, Micah colluding with men in power or men with money shouldn't have surprised me. He was an opportunist through and through.

"All I want to do is get this behind me so I can graduate in May like I'm supposed to."

"Good," Dean Muller said. "Once we are done here I'll cancel the hearing and you'll have to do some community service and that's it." He looked over at Micah. "Mr. Williams, it's your show, young man."

Micah smiled at the man and then looked at me. "Take off your clothes."

I stared at him blankly for a moment. It was clear what they expected. I'd used my body for less important things and as much as I loathed the idea of submitting to Micah, I had little choice. My eyes stayed on Micah as I stripped down to my boxers. I was about to say something when Micah handed Dean Muller his phone. They planned on documenting the whole ordeal.

"Malcolm is going to record our little session. He likes to watch and have video to look over later. Just something he likes."

The explanation was unnecessary since I was sure Micah would use the video for something else. Bribery wasn't out of play in Micah's book. I thrust my boxers down and stepped out of my last piece of clothing.

Micah walked up to me. A sadistic smile curved his lips as he ran the tips of his fingers over my chest down to my abs. As much as I hated what was going on my body couldn't help but respond. Micah squeezed my thickening manhood and looked me in the face.

"You never disappoint," Micah said. "Been a while but I still remember how hot our little freak sessions could get. Help me put on a show for the old man so we can get out of here and handle some real business."

I looked over at Dean Muller. He had his dick in his hand, stroking as he leered at Micah and I. Time seemed to slow to a crawl. It was like I was outside of my body, just watching everything unfold. I felt a heavy hand go to my shoulder and push me down.

Without being told, I unfastened Micah's jeans and took his limp dick in my mouth. The deacon's son moaned when I took the length of him to my throat and dragged my tongue over his balls. I looked up at him seductively, playing my role, and watched as he pulled his shirt over his head.

Micah's body flexed and tensed. His hips slowly grinded against my face. Giving his growing meat purpose. Our eyes locked as he gradually worked up a rhythm, fucking my face. If the circumstances were different and I didn't have Keith on my mind, the scene would have been hot as Hell. The only time I would get off with clients was when they watched me with someone else. Being objectified like that was a fantasy of mine. But this was a sad perversion of that desire.

"Swallow that dick," Micah commanded. "Keith will never know that you were on your knees sucking my dick as long as you keep your mouth shut."

Anger bubbled in my gut. The urge to clamp down and bite the boy's dick teased the muscles of my jaw. It was a fleeting thought. My eyes moved to Dean Muller. He was getting off on the spectacle before him. I spotted his wedding band when he reached up and pulled at his nipple.

Micah pulled his dick from my mouth and slapped the heavy, spit covered meat across my lips. He dragged the tip of his dick across the side of my face, smearing a stream of precum on my cheek. Hunger burned in his eyes. I knew what he wanted.

I stood up and looked at him. Hate and lust blazed in my eyes. I knew he saw it but was equally sure that it only made him hornier. Slowly, I turned and walked over to Dean Muller's desk. I climbed up, bent over and exposed my hole for Micah's inspection.

I looked over my shoulder and watched Micah yank off the rest of his clothes. His body was on point. I hated to admit it, but the sight of him naked turned my on. My dick jumped and smacked my stomach. My hole twitched in anticipation. No one in all my years of illicit sex had tongued my hole like Micah.

Like a sex god, Micah strolled up to my ass. He surveyed the prize he had extorted for a moment. Then I felt his rough hands firmly grip my mounds, squeezing each cheek for good measure. He ran the side of his palm down the crack of my ass. The smooth but hard texture of his flesh burned against my rosebud. He was working my body and I loved it.

"You remember the first time I bent you over," Micah asked. He spit on my hole and poked my entrance with his finger. "You were so scared. You were shaking so hard that you almost fell off my bed. But when I tasted you for the very first time…your body just melted in my mouth."

I swallowed hard. He was right. As teenagers we played grab ass and even compared our dicks. But one night, when I stayed over, he convinced me to strip. Micah had bent me over and literally kissed my ass. He had no idea that eating ass involved more tongue than lips at the time but he was dedicated to the task.

Micah leaned forward and blew a stream of cool breath over my hole. My body shuddered. My ass twitched. Then he did something that had always drove me crazy. Micah pried my cheeks apart and started whispering to my ass.

I could never hear what he said. It was something he started doing after the first time he fucked me. I'd asked him what he said but he always told me that what was said was between him and my ass.

He kissed my puckered hole and then dived in. His tongue worked hard and fast, breaking the tightness of my sphincter with little effort. My mind drifted away as my body got caught up in the rapture of lust and physical need.

"Eat that ass," I moaned. "Oh my God, you feel so fucking good!"

Micah ate my hole like a savage beast. His tongue, lips and teeth worked in tandem to bring mind blowing pleasure to my ass. It was sloppy and messy but so fucking good. His hands gripped at my cheeks, forcing them further and further apart so he could drive his tongue deeper. Then he sucked at my hole and pulled away with a loud pop.

"Come down and bend that ass over," he ordered between labored breaths. His rugged voice hinted at the carnal lust beckoning both or bodies. "Got my dick leaking, ready to feel that ass."

Micah pressed hard on the small of my back with one hand and smacked my ass with the other. My flesh jiggled just enough for the vibration to ripple through my body and prime my spirit for what lay ahead.

His hardness burned against my flesh. Micah dragged his swollen head over my wet hole and grinded until I felt the slickness of his precum lube my fuck chute. His nails dug into my waist. I could feel his dick poke angrily at my entrance, demanding access. Sweet pain shot through my body when I tried to push back on his dick. My body wanted him inside but demanded patience.

Micah swiveled his head back and forth, slow stroking my tight hole. Pressure built firm and fast until that agonizing moment when his head eased into my bowels. I clawed at the desk and pressed my face against the wood grain. My mind screamed for me to run but my hole steeled my body and commanded me to submit.

I squirmed like a child getting a shot as Micah's thick inches plunged to the depths of my bowels. Half his pole slinked inside me when I felt him press against my prostate. My dick hardened. My ass clenched tightly against the foreign invader. My legs shook violently. I struggled to take in a breath but my throat only constricted in blissful agony.

"Grip that shit with those tight ass fucking walls, nigga," Micah said, growly the words. He leaned over, pressed his chest against my back and snaked deeper in the pit of my gut. "I'm going to fuck you hard and deep. Aint felt this ass in a long time. Make sure you don't run. I want you to take every stroke like the dick hungry pro you fucking are.

Moans rumbling from my gut were only way I could acknowledge his words. He felt so hard and raw inside me. My nerve ending tortured my pain and pleasure receptors. I felt like puddy being molded by his fuck tool.

"Fuck him," Dean Muller said, his voice harsh. "Fuck the shit out of his little ass."

Micah pulled back until only the head violated

my hole. His meat jumped and then slide back in my special place, rigid and throbbing. The strokes were slow and purposeful at first. My ass creamed all over his dick. I could feel precum oozing from my shaft. He was literally fucking the nutt out of me. My head thrashed and my arms wailed in the air. It was too much.

"Fuck this ass!" It took a moment for it to register that it was me speaking. "Beat that shit the fuck in like you own it!"

Micah's body hardened along with his dick. He gripped me by the waist and fucked me like a porn star. I threw my ass back, meeting each body crushing stroke he hurled against my hole. Our sweaty flesh collided with primal intent. I got dizzy from all the effort and the short breaths I sucked in between strokes.

His powerful, measured strokes quickly gave way to a frenzied humping. I could feel his dick thicken and harden against my ass walls. He grunted and groaned, unable to contain himself. Micah was about to flood my hole.

Cum erupted from my dick the second I heard that orgasmic moan rumble over Micah's lips. I felt his hot seed slam against my prostate and line my abused walls. His dick jumped over and over again. Nutt oozed from my open hole, down my leg and he was still coming.

Finally, Micah collapsed atop my sweaty covered back and hugged me. His dick flopped from my hole along with a cup full of cum. He bit at my ear and hummed a moan of pure satisfaction.

"I'm sorry for this and all that shit that happened back at Thanksgiving," he said. "Keith hurt me. Seeing him with you just put me in a crazy place. I'm sorry. It's too bad that it had to come to this for us to fuck again."

I pulled away from his embrace and stood up, leaning against the dean's desk. I looked over at the college administrator. He was cleaning the mess he'd made on his slacks. I assumed that he was satisfied. My gaze found its way back to Micah. He was staring at, still naked and covered in sweat. Cum dripped from his slowly deflating manhood.

"Dean Muller," I called out tentatively. "Are we done?"

The married official nodded his head and waved. He was busy adjusting his dick and fixing his clothes. The show was over and it was back to business. I shot Micah a hard stare but didn't say a word to him. I quickly got dressed and was out the door the moment the dean said it was okay to leave. Micah was right on my hills the moment I began descending the stairs in front of the college administrative building.

"I'm the one that should be mad," Micah said. "You were fucking around with Keith for years behind my back. You know he's the reason why I dropped out of school. You was like a brother."

"How did you even get out of jail? Aren't you supposed to going to trial for stabbing me in your parent's front yard?"

"I'm going to get the charges dropped."

I tripped over my feet. "How you going to pull that off? You know the DA? The two of you have some sexual arrangement?"

"He's not gay. But he is cheating on his wife with a paralegal in his office. But none of that matters. You're going to help me get the charges dropped. You owe me that much."

I stopped mid-stride. "Are you really that fucking delusional? Micah, you stabbed me. You could have killed me. Why the fuck would I do anything to help you?"

"You of all people should be able to appreciate how what happened was an accident. We were really close at one point. I told you things that I've never told anyone else. I cried on your shoulder almost every night when I was going through that shit with Keith. Can you really stand here, knowing how he hurt me, and not understand why I did what I did?"

I looked at Micah. I couldn't believe that I was actually considering what he'd said as a good reason for what he'd done to me. He cut me with a knife and had me in the hospital for weeks. As bad as I felt about dealing with the man that crushed him emotionally, I just couldn't bring myself to forgive him.

"There's no excuse for what you did," I said plainly. "I want nothing to do with you. And I'll be there at the trial. When I take the stand, I'm going to look you straight in the eye when I describe the weeks I spent in the hospital."

Micah nodded. "If that's how you want to play it, fine. Just realize that your little blog and that video of you fucking at Discreet Encounters is only the tip of the iceberg. I know shit and get dirt on you that would have your life fucked."

"You're a little evil motherfucker. How did we ever become friends? Micah, you're worst than the lowest lowlife. You'll have to atone for your sins."

"I'm sure when that time comes I'll still have no regrets. I was hoping that it didn't come to this. I like you. I really do. Hell, fucking you a minute ago made me remember how much I wanted to be with you and make you my dude at one point in time."

"It's never going to happen," I scoffed. "That shit back there was just business."

"I know. Just like I know that you're a big fan of that type of business." Micah licked his lips and gave me a knowing look. "After this trial shit blows over you won't ever have to deal with me. You can run off into the sunset with your dude and his openly gay ass. Happily ever after and all that shit."

"You really think I'm worried about your little bribes, nigga? Fuck you! I'll take my chances in court."

"What about your father? Do you think he'll be ass forgiving and accepting as me and my brothers? You don't think he'll do the exact same thing my parents did? All we have is each other. I need you to try and forgive me. I love you like my own brother, Jabari."

I smiled. "Is this another one of your little manipulation tricks? You should have stayed in school and took up psychology. You'd have made a lot of fucking money. But that shit won't work on me. You're not my friend. You're not like family. You're a leech, Micah. You suck the life from everyone around you. And now that I see you for what you are, I'm done."

"Fine. What about that book? You're ready to let your father's legacy be destroyed."

"Kareem is the one publishing the book. There isn't a thing any of us can do to stop it from coming out."

"You must not know who you're talking to. I can stop the book and all the pictures from ever seeing the light of day."

"Go for it," I said plainly. "I'm sure everyone involved, including your brother Isaiah, will appreciate the effort."

"You're the one that introduced my brother to the boy. Don't tell me that you don't feel the least bit guilty about him getting photos taken. What about Tasha? Your cousin? Don't give a fuck about any of them, do you?"

"There's nothing I can do."

"Help me stop Kareem from putting out the book."

"Why do you think we can stop that man from releasing that fucking book?" I asked, frustration souring my voice. "He probably has a team of publishers and editors who have access to the book. You can't just delete it from his laptop and be done."

Micah smiled. "Come to Chapel Hill with me. Everything will make more sense when we get there. Trust me."

I looked at my one-time best friend warily. I didn't trust him as far as I could throw him. He was bribing me not to testify against him and soliciting my help to stop a book that would destroy my father's church. Hate rumbled in my gut. That was the problem with Micah. Sometimes he was the most selfish person in the world and other times he would put everything on the line for the people he loved. Now, I was scared what he might do to Kareem.

"Fine," I answered. "Follow me back to my apartment so I can drop off my car. I'm guessing you walk all the way from Charlotte to Richmond."

Micah grinned and pulled out a set of car keys. He clicked the button and a Mercedes-Benz SLK beeped over in the parking lot. I shook my head not even wanting to think who's car he was driving. I went to my car and peeled out from the parking lot with Micah following behind me.

I watched Micah in my rearview mirror the whole trip. I thought that I was over his conniving ass but the more I looked back at him the more the memories of all the things we did together, usually the for the time, came rushing back. His seed leaking from my ass wasn't helping either.

When I made it to the complex I waved for him to park in one of the visitor spots outside the gate. I really didn't want him to know which apartment was mine. He backed into the spot but pulled right out when pressed the gate code and went through. I was too annoyed to even care. I whipped my car around the turns and pulled up to my building. Keith was right there, leaned up against a Bentley.

I almost pumped the brakes so hard that Micah damn near slammed into me. I looked up in the rearview mirror. Micah's eyes were right on Keith. Every curse word imaginable crossed my mind. The last thing I needed was for the two of them to see one another again. Micah would lose his shit and there was no telling what Keith might do. He'd gotten a gun license after Micah attacked me.

I pulled up a few spots away between two cars, praying that Micah got the hint and didn't pull in near me. My heart pounded against my chest and sweat drenched my shit as I saw Micah drive by my car. He kept driving and parked two buildings down. A sigh of relief shook my soul.

As soon as I stepped out Keith walked towards me and said, "Hey babe! Surprised?"

"What are you doing here?" I asked, still nervously looking towards where Micah parked. I said about a dozen prayers in my mind asking that he stay in the car. "I thought you was supposed to be performing in London or something."

"I flew over right quick for a show I have in

DC. Wanted to stop by and see how my baby was doing. I miss you like crazy. This long distance shit is killing me. Was thinking about canceling the rest of the shows in Europe."

"No you're not. You're living your dream."

"Without you," he said, cutting me off. "Not having you in my arms when I wake up is pure torture." He walked towards me, biting his bottom lip. "Plus, I'm getting a lot of offered for shows here in the states after I came out."

Keith leaned in to kiss me but I planted my hand on his chest and said, "You might be open and free but I'm not. My father is still the reverend of a big ass church and people are always watching me."

"Then why we still standing outside? Let's go up to your apartment and reunite like we supposed to."

"When is your show?" I asked. I glanced over my shoulder to make sure Micah didn't make an appearance. "I was about to head down to see my dad. There's a lot of shit going on that just popped up and I want to make sure he's okay."

"You okay," Keith asked. "You're acting like someone is following you." He grinned at me reassuringly. "Look, I saw all that shit about the book. No one even knows who's church they're talking about yet. The paparazzi aren't going to come out the woodwork yet. Relax. And my show is tomorrow night."

"You're right," I replied, playing off my nervousness. "Come on, you can visit for a second while I pack a duffle bag. I can drive up to DC for the show and give you the one on one time you deserve."

He smiled at me as I walked by and then smacked my ass. It would have been hot if Micah seeing it wasn't on my mind. I trotted up the stairs and swooped into my apartment like a whirlwind. I needed to get in and out as quickly as possible. I knew how Micah's mind worked. He would give me some leeway but if I had him waiting too long there would be Hell to pay.

I bolted for the bedroom but Keith's strong arms wrapped around my waist and pulled me back into his tight grip. He felt so good against my body. I closed my eyes and tried to pull away. It hurt so much to deny the man I loved what he craved. What I craved.

"Slow the fuck down," he moaned in my ear.

"I see you've been busy."

I frowned and opened my eyes. My lube, Fleshlight and dildo were still on the bed. They had been there for a couple days and hadn't been put to use since I was contacted by Dean Muller. I had been too depressed to clean anything in the apartment.

"You been getting that ass open for daddy?" Keith asked. His rough hands moved to my pant button and quickly popped it open. My jeans were wrapped around my thighs before I could think. "I know you in a rush but you have to let me feel you for just a second. I promise on everything I won't take long.

I moaned, longing to feel him inside of me but it felt so wrong. "I can't. I need to get on the road, Keith. Come on, I'll let you do everything you want when I get to DC." I clenched at the door frame but Keith's grip only tightened. He ripped my underwear and dragged his finger over my recently used hole. "Baby, stop. Please."

"You already wet as fuck and open," he growled in my ear. I could feel his raw flesh poke at my hole. "You've never made me wait before. I'm so horny I'm sure I won't last more than a minute."

I tried to fight him off but my body refused to work with me. Keith shoved his hard dick up my ass with one thrust of his hips. I saw lights. My finger nails dug into the wall holding the door frame. He was so hard and rough. It hurt like fuck but the spontaneity of the moment had me caught up, legs shaking and all.

Keith didn't make love this time. He just fucked me. He went on and on about how wet my ass was. Each time I heard the words my chest squeezed from guilt. My ass was so wet and open because Micah had just fucked me. I couldn't believe what I was doing.

"Don't fight me, baby," he moaned between hunches. "I'm so fucking close."

I could feel his dick unload in my ass the moment he uttered the last words. I felt dirty as fuck. The man I dreamed of spending the rest of my life with had just busted a nut in my ass right after Micah. I didn't deserve him.

"That was hot. But I have to get on the road."

Keith wiped the sweat from his forehead and smiled. "Alright, nigga. Come give your man a kiss and I'll let you pack."

I gave him a peck on the lips and trifled through my drawers and closet. By the time Keith had pulled his pants back up and caught his breath I was packed. I hurried him to the door, looked back and made sure I wasn't forgetting anything. Keith just looked at me, laughing.

"What's so funny?" I asked, somewhat annoyed.

"You." He held up my keys and grinned. "They were on the dresser."

I snatched my keys and gave him a playful evil eye. I shook my head and pulled the door open. Micah was standing right there, less than a foot away, and I was the only thing between him and Keith, the love of his life that was forever lost to him.

Eye For An Eye

I looked over Jabari's shoulder and eyeballed Keith. Unwavering contempt hardened my face. All I could over the man was a cold, stoic stare. I wasn't going to let him see the hurt that still strangled my heart written all over my face. Being that weak near him wasn't an option. Years marred in pain and tears passed before I was strong enough to no longer give a damn about Keith. Now, I would face him with my head held high.

"What the fuck is he doing here?!?" Keith yanked Jabari behind him and balled his fists. "Try something and I promise I'm going to fuck you up, Micah. I swear to God I will drop you right here, right now."

"Why so damn, serious?" I asked. I frowned at him, tauntingly. "Can't we try to be adults for once? Act like we can get along."

Confusion wrinkled Keith's smooth forehead. He looked back at Jabari and asked, "What the fuck is he talking about? How does he even know where you live?"

"He…I…Well," Jabari stammered. He closed his eyes and took a deep breath. "Micah talked to the dean for me. Something came up and they were about to expel me."

Keith swiveled his head back to me. "You trying to get my man to drop the charges against you?"

It felt like a needle pierced my heart when Keith said 'my man.' My lip twitched as I said, "I'm trying to do what needs to be done to put all this behind us. I can go and live my life and you two can finally do what you'll been doing behind closed doors out in the open."

"Fuck that," Keith scoffed. His chest heaved in anger. "We not about to get manipulated by your ass. You fucked up and now you got to deal with the motherfucking consequences."

Jabari pulled at Keith's arm. He yanked him a

step back inside the apartment and spoke to the man in hushed tones. His eyes kept darting back to me. He and I both knew that he had to get Keith on a leash before or my tongue would start moving. Nothing would have made me happier than to show Keith the video of me fucking *his man* less than an hour ago.

After what seemed like an eternity, Keith turned towards me and asked, "How the fuck you going to stop a publishing company from putting a book out?"

"You know me well enough to know that I can make shit happen that other niggas couldn't," I said, crossing my arms over my chest. "You really want to sit here and question me about my capabilities? You of all people should know I can always pull a trick out from my ass when it really matters."

Keith rolled his eyes and looked back to Jabari. "You can't trust this nigga. A couple months ago he stabbed you. He'll fuck you over the first chance he gets. The book is going to come out no matter what. I don't care what this nigga says, aint no way to stop the shit."

Hope drained from Jabari's face as he looked

up at Keith. I could see the defeat overwhelming his spirit. A few moments ago my former best friend was ready to hop on the road and make some moves. Now, he looked like the world was coming to an end.

"What would it hurt to try," I asked. "If it's going to come out either way why not try instead of just sitting here and waiting for the ball to fucking drop? Worse that can happen is we make a trip to Chapel Hill and come right back with empty hands."

Jabari slowly began to nod. He looked at Keith and said, "Baby, I'll be back in time to see your show in DC. It shouldn't take long."

"He should come," I suggested. I looked at Keith, plotting exactly how I could put his ass to work. "We'll make it a bona fide road trip."

"Fine," Keith barked. He looked me up and down. "I'll drive. Not like we can all fit in that Roadster you're pushing. What old man let you hold his whip anyways? Did it cost him one or two blowjobs?"

I held on to the smile on my face for dear life. The last thing I wanted to do was give his ass the satisfaction of knowing that he could still get to me. I didn't even offer his ass a reply. I motioned for the two them to lead the way to Keith's car.

We piled in the car; Keith drove, Jabari sat in the front seat and I sat in the middle of the backseat. I leaned back, enjoyed how spacious and nice the car was. I'd been in most luxury vehicles but never a Bentley. I leaned up between the happy couple.

"Is the car yours or are you borrowing it for some video shoot or some shit?"

"Why, you want one?" Keith looked up at the rearview mirror. "You'd have to suck a lot of dick and actually take it up the ass more than few times before you could afford it."

"It's always easy to flex when the shit aint yours, hunh?" I turned my phone around so Keith and Jabari could see the picture I pulled up. "Your producer is pretty popular on Instagram. Ya'll must be really close for him to let you use his Bentley. Hell, I had to turn him down when he got referred by a friend of mine. He's a little too kinky for my taste."

Jabari frowned as he looked from me to Keith. I leaned back and tried to enjoy the show. Surprisingly, Jabari didn't say a word. He gave

Keith a look and sunk down in his seat. They obviously weren't the type that argued in front of other people. That didn't work for me. I wanted to see sparks fire.

"Where exactly are we going?" Keith asked, breaking the awkward silence. "And what exactly are you going to do to the guy when we see him? I hope you're not going to do anything stupid. I'm not going to jail for you, Micah."

"We're going to Chapel Hill. Take I-95 to I-85 and ride until he get close to Durham. I'll give you more directions when we almost there. And don't worry about how shit is going to work out. I'm still putting shit in place. Just know that I'm going to need you to help as well."

Keith shook his head. "Man, I'm here for the ride. I'm not getting involved in any crazy shit you got going on."

"You haven't changed at all, have you?" The words came out without any thought. "You're so fucking selfish. You're so quick to pass judgment even when someone does something that not only helps them but helps you."

"Don't start with me, Micah. I promise you won't like shit that I say."

"Fuck it, we going to be in this fucking for a good little minute. May as well get everything out."

"Fine. What you need to know that you don't already? I stopped fucking with you because you're a slut. You tricked out your body for money and came back to my bed like aint shit happen. You played me."

"So I was playing you when I paid for your tuition when you lost your basketball scholarship? You do remember how much that shit cost, right? I'm not going to apologize for shit that I've done. Men gave me money for shit since I was like 16. I stopped when I went to school. Even passed some shit up when I got to Virginia so I could focus on class then on you when we started chilling together."

Jabari perked up on the last comment. He knew I was talking about Discreet Encounters. I was the one that put him on with one of the guys who worked there after I was approached. I would have been dicking down straight niggas in front of their bitches just like Jabari if I didn't pass on it for Keith's whack ass.

"I didn't ask you to pay for my school," he

said, coldly. "You did that shit on your own. I was grateful. You know that. But you the one that couldn't stop. And my dumb ass didn't ask any fucking questions when all that money started rolling in."

"You right. When we were taking trips to New York and Miami on the weekends you didn't say a damn thing. I drop a thousand on your wardrobe and you'd give me some ass, no questions asked. I was the one that got you your first keyboard and a laptop with all that editing software for your music."

"You want me to pay you back for all the shit you did?" he asked. Keith pulled out a wad of cash and tossed back in my lap. "That's ten stacks. Consider it my first of four installments."

I held the cash in my hand. I wanted to throw it at his ass but I wasn't about to be a stupid nigga over a broken heart and some dick and ass. I put the money in my pocket. I was sure it would come in handy once we made it to Chapel Hill.

"It's a start," I said. "But you can never pay back all the years of hurt I went through over your ass. I was in love with you. First man to ever have my fucking heart. And you just walked away like I was nothing. And then I find out you started dealing with my best friend. Nigga, you lucky you wasn't the one on the other end of my blade."

"Don't sit there and threaten me, Micah." He looked back at me for a moment and then back on the road. "I thought you was slinging dope or some shit. Not ass and dick to the highest fucking bidder. When I found your second phone with all those men asking to spend time with you I was done. I didn't have a thing to say to your ass."

"I did that shit for you," I whispered. "Everything I did was for you."

"No," Keith shook his head. "You're sick, Micah. You're addicted to sex and money. You get a rush from being that close to men with power. The fact that they desire you only makes it more intense for you. I read the messages between you and your little home girl that you told everything to. You not about to lie to me."

"Fuck you. Don't sit there and try to judge me. Act like I'm the only one doing shit behind closed doors to make shit easier for you."

"Don't, Micah," Jabari said. "Just stop. Ya'll done said enough."

Keith frowned. "Naw, let the prostitute talk." He turned and looked at me. "What other sins do you want to confess so that I can forgive you? Since that's obviously what you want."

"Why the Hell would I need forgiveness for some shit I'm not ashamed about? Especially when *your man* does the same shit."

"What the fuck you talking about," Keith asked, anger laced in his voice. He turned towards Jabari. "Tell me that nigga is lying or I promise to God I'm going to—"

"Going to what, nigga?" I asked. "Put your hands on my brother and I'll fucking kill you. Yea, those days of you putting your hands on a motherfucker is over. Self hating faggot. Drive the car and shut the fuck up before I call that ugly, fat ass producer and promise his some dick if he tells me all about your ass."

Keith gripped the steering wheel, his forearms taut and hard. I could see the muscles flexed and strained under his skin. I didn't care. If he wanted to throw down I was ready. Never again would a man put his hands on me without whipping his ass too.

My head hunkered down but I could see the

look on Jabari's face reflecting off the passenger side window. I had told him almost everything that happened between me and Keith. All the times he would curse me out for being gay after we had sex. How he said some of the most hurtful things imaginable only to be sweet as lemonade the next minute. That's why I spent money on him like I did. To minimize the bad times because I loved him. I loved him so much that I never told anyone, including Jabari, how he would beat me.

No one else said a word the rest of the ride. Although the space between Jabari and Keith was the same they seemed more distant. There was a chilly air between them. I hated being spiteful but I was happy that Jabari had finally seen Keith for the piece of shit he was.

"Go ahead and take the next exit," I said, leaning forward. "We need to make a quick stop to pick someone up."

"You really think it's smart to get more people involved in whatever it is we're going to do?"

"Damn, you sound like we're going to kill the boy or something." An eerie quiet fell in the car. "We're not going to kill, Kadeem. I'm a lot of things but I'm not a murderer. The boy just needs to be given a choice."

"And what if he makes the wrong choice?" Keith asked. He sounded super skeptical. "You can't make a man do something he doesn't want to do. If this Kadeem guy is committed to putting the book out you can't stop him. It won't matter what you bribe him with."

"Like I said before we left, it won't hurt to try." I pointed at the street coming up. "Go ahead and turned down that street."

We followed the winding path to a huge mansion sitting on about dozen acres of land. Even Keith, with his pseudo celebrity status, was impressed with the house. His eyes went big but his mouth stayed shut, unlike Jabari's. I pulled out my cell phone.

"I'm here little, nigga. Go ahead and buzz me in before I have to beat that ass."

The twelve foot tall gate opened and Keith drove up to the roundabout in front of the house. Our host came out the front door and skipped down the staircase like the big ass kid he was. I bolted from the car and ran to him. He wrapped his arms around me and planted his lips on mine like we were long lost lovers.

Siph pulled away and giggled. "Damn dude, it's good to see your ass. Been missing you."

I rubbed my knee against his hardening dick. "I see. I don't know why you don't just got out and date. I'm sure a lot of guys would love to get with you. Once they feel that tight Asian hole they'd be hooked."

"I'm half black too, Micah. Don't play me. You know I got that nigga dick."

I laughed and shook my head. I didn't see them but I looked back over my shoulder and saw my traveling companions. "This is Jabari and that's Keith. These are the two guys who are going to help me with my little plan. Did you get all the stuff I asked you for?"

"Yea. The guy that I contracted for my office building security system brought over all the stuff like fifteen minutes ago. Cost a pretty penny, too."

I reached in my pocket and tossed him the wad of cash Keith had thrown at me. "Hope that covers it."

Siph sucked his teeth. "Do you not see the mansion or the three Phantom Rolls Royce's in my driveway? Do I look like I need money? You already know what I want."

"Yea, some time with your best friend," I said teasingly. "But I told you we were in a rush. Time is working against us. If we don't move now, none of this shit is going to matter."

"That's cool. You can do a little down payment right now." Siph looked over my shoulder and smiled. "I want him. Just to suck my dick right quick. You know I nutt fast, Micah. Come on."

I looked over and saw he was talking about Keith. "Let me see what I can do."

Jabari would have been easier to convince. With Keith in his mood and on his high horse I was sure he'd say no. Siph was cool as fuck but when he set his sights on something he had to have it. He wouldn't take no for an answer. He'd go back to playing his video games instead of helping me with my Kadeem problem. I walked up to Keith and Jabari.

"I need you to take one for the team, Keith. Siph wants you. That's the only way he'll help us."

"The fuck? You just gave that nigga ten grand.

I'm not about to sell my body for some bullshit. What the fuck is he going to do that we can't do on our own?"

"He got some surveillance equipment that he's going to use to catch Kadeem doing something he shouldn't be doing. My plan isn't going to work unless we get his help. His little ass is smart as fuck. He's only twenty years old and already a multi-millionaire. He makes game apps for smart phones. Works like one day out the week now."

"What does he want?" Jabari asked. "Maybe he'll let me do whatever it is that he's asking."

I shook my head. "When Siph asks for something, there are no negotiations. He's spoiled rotten but has no problem not getting what he wants, he'll just not give us what we need."

"You didn't answer his question," Keith said. "What exactly does he want me to do?"

"Just head."

Keith shrugged. "Fuck it, he can suck my dick until he's blue in the face."

"Actually, he wants you to suck his dick. He's a little dude but he got some meat. Shit is pretty too. And he nuts a lot."

"Alright," Keith waved me off, "I don't need a

sex resume for the man. Do we even have time to do this shit?"

"I was about to tell you that Siph doesn't take long to cum, but you aint want his resume."

Keith shook his head. He cut his eyes from me and looked at Jabari. Words weren't exchanged but it was clear that an agreement had been made. I watched Keith walk towards Siph. They said a few words and suddenly, Siph yanked his pants and underwear down to his ankles.

"Shit," Jabari cursed. "He's going to do that shit right here?"

"I mean, he has all the privacy he needs with all this land. And he knows we're in a rush. Plus I bet he's getting off on the fact that we're watching."

"How did you meet this dude anyways?"

I looked over at Jabari. "I don't spend all my time tricking off and bullshitting around. Last year I went to a hacker's convention. He was holding a seminar. I made sure I met him at the end of the session. We flew back here that same night. He has a helicopter in the back."

"Hmm, not as much a fuck up as everyone thinks. Online classes, hacking into people shit and rubbing shoulders with millionaires. I'm impressed."

"You shouldn't be. I just do what I need to do for me. You need to be thinking about whether or not you think being with Keith is the best thing for you. You haven't met the real Keith yet, but when you do…"

"Don't worry about me, Micah. I'll be fine."

I gave him a sidelong glance and shook my head. I turned and faced Siph and Keith. Watching them was half funny and half hot as fuck. Siph was short as shit and Keith was tall as fuck. Watching Siph pump his dick in and out Keith's mouth while on his tippy toes was a sight to see. Luckily, it didn't last long.

"I knew he would swallow," I whispered. Jabari frowned at his boyfriend. "Siph tastes good as fuck."

Keith got off his knees, gave Siph a look and walked back to Jabari, wiping his lips. I smiled at Keith, knowing that he enjoyed the public oral gratification he'd just given to Siph. Before I could say a word, Siph was urging us inside the mansion. We didn't have much time to explore and enjoy all that the man's home had to offer.

We went and got the surveillance equipment and was back out the door, piled up in one of Siph's Phantoms, heading out.

"You trying to pull some weak ass sting on this guy," Keith asked from the backseat. "What do you think you're going to catch him doing that would make him give up publishing the book?"

"Let me worry about that. You just help out when you can. Cause we're going to need you. Kadeem knows me and Jabari. He doesn't know you. You're going to be the bait, Keith."

I texted my cop friend that I had tailing Kadeem to find out where he was. And, as usual, he was downtown at one of the pubs popular with the college crowd. The boy loved to drink. I just hoped that he was as open to linking up with Keith as he was with trying to get drunk.

Kadeem was where I needed him to be. My cop buddy was posted and ready to move when I said. I looked back at Keith. He looked like he was ready to trap the wannabe novelist. Now, all we needed was a room and the last little piece of the puzzle. I took out my phone and call in for a hotel reservation.

"I just sent you a text message with pictures of

Kadeem," I said to Keith. I passed him a small vial. "Put this in his drink and get him back to the hotel we're about to get. It's not a date rape drug. It will just get him horny as Hell."

"I get him to the room and then what?" Keith asked. He frowned. "How the fuck did you get my number?"

"You worrying about the wrong shit right now. When you get him to the room go as far as you feel comfortable going. I'll make my move when I know he's ready."

"Whatever man. I still don't think the shit will work." He looked over at Jabari. "I'm going to try, babe. But don't get your hopes up. This shit might not end how you want to end."

We pulled up in front of the bar and Keith hopped out. He had to do his part and we had to do ours. I checked in at the Hyatt down the street. We needed two rooms. Once I got the keycards I left one at the desk for Keith. I made sure to text him about the key as Siph, Jabari and I hauled the equipment up to the room where Keith would bring Kadeem.

We place about a half dozen small ass cameras and microphones all around the room. We needed to catch every angle and record every sound. Once that was done we went to the makeshift surveillance room and set up the flat screen monitors.

"Now what," Jabari asked. He looked over at all the equipment and nodded. "We just wait?"

"Pretty much. Can't make a move until Keith comes back to the hotel with Kadeem."

"I'm sure we can find something to do while we wait," Siph said. He motioned towards the bed. "Be a shame to waste a nice, king sized bed."

I grinned at him and then looked at Jabari. Slowly, a horny smile covered his face. The three of us stripped down as quickly as possible. We were on the bed kissing and sucking like there was no tomorrow. I was surprised that Jabari even entertained Siph's little suggestion. But I wasn't about to complain.

Siph was riding my dick shortly after a bottle of lube appeared. His tight hole squeezed the length of my pole like no other. I didn't have time to linger on the incredible sensations teasing my dick. Jabari had my legs in the air, pushing his slickened manhood against my hole.

I was like old times when Jabari and I tag

teamed dudes. Now, he was getting his turn since I had fucked him earlier. It was cool. The three of us didn't last long. About ten minutes past when I felt Siph's ass clench my dick. I looked down and saw his dick jerk and squirt a fountain of cum. I nutted right in his ass and Jabari skeeted in mine.

We all jumped in the shower and had a heavy petting and kissing session. Shit was hot. When we finally pulled our hands from one another we stepped out the bathroom, each toweling off our body. There was movement on the screen. Finally, Keith and Kadeem had made it back to the hotel.

"Are you recording?" I asked, gripping Siph's shoulder. "We can't miss this."

He nodded. "It's been recording since I turned the screens on." Siph looked back at me and asked, "why are we recording this part? I thought another guy was coming."

"Why are you recording this, Micah?" Jabari crossed his arms over his bare chest. "You can't extort everyone in the world with fucking videos of them having sex."

"I'm not going to extort Keith. There aint shit

that I want from him. Just sit back and watch and you can decide when it's all over what to do with the video."

Jabari looked at me with distrust and suspicion. He finished toweling off and got dress. So did Siph and I. We all huddled around the screens and watched the spectacle unfolding just a few rooms down. The little potion my drug dealer back in Charlotte made me was working perfectly. Kadeem moved like a mad man.

Keith didn't look like he had a problem keeping up. The two of them were naked just moments after they stepped into the room. Kadeem threw Jabari's boyfriend on the bed. He looked down at him and then slowly crawled between his legs. Keith's head thrust back as his dick disappeared in Kadeem's mouth.

I looked at Jabari from the corner of my eye. He watched the screen, obviously upset. I tried to feel bad but offering my sympathy didn't even make sense. Jabari had done worse and for money. I guess watching it was different than knowing. Either way, I figured now was as good a time as any to bring in the final piece. I pulled out my phone.

"Go ahead," I said into the receiver. "It's time."

Jabari and Siph both looked at me, curiosity twinkling in their gaze. I grinned and glued my face to one of the screens. Only moments went by before the door to Keith and Kadeem's hotel room swung open. My surprise guest was naked and headed for the bed before either of them could complain.

"Who is that, Micah?" Jabari asked. Concern lingered in his voice. "He looks young as fuck."

"He is," I confirmed. "He's only 15."

"What the fuck is wrong with you?!? Are you crazy?"

"What else did you think was going to happen? Was there anything else that we could record him doing that would be enough to get him to stop publishing the book?"

"So you want to make the boy a pedophile? That shit is sick. I can't watch this."

"Then don't. But I'm sure the DA would love to see it. And they boy's father, who happens to be the head basketball coach at UNC."

Jabari just shook his head. He walked over to the window and stood there until it was all over.

It didn't surprise me that Keith stayed the whole time. Now, he was just as exposed at Kadeem. My little friend stayed long enough with Kadeem after Keith left so we had video and audio if I decided to just use the video with Kadeem and the fifteen year-old.

When Keith got back to the room I told him some bullshit story about the guy who came in and jumped into a ménage a trois with him and Kadeem. Siph finished packing up and offered them a ride back to his place. I was staying. Had to seal the deal with Kadeem. I pulled Jabari to the side before he left the room.

"Leave him before it's too late."

"Don't tell what to do, Micah." Jabari tried to walk away but I took him by the arm. "What do you want? We came down here and did what you wanted. It might work it might not. But you helping out doesn't give you the right to tell me what to do."

"He's going to hurt you," I warned. "It's only a matter of time."

"Whatever. Don't think all that went down to today changes anything. I'll do whatever it is you want me to do for the DA to drop the assault charges. After that, I'm done. You go ahead and destroy the copies of the book at the publisher and make sure Kadeem doesn't publish that book."

I pursed my lips and looked at Jabari. Our friendship was officially over. I let go of his arm and watch him walk to the end of the hall where Keith and Siph waited. I wondered if he was going to tell Keith who the boy was and how old he was. It didn't matter. It was time to finish what I'd started.

I went to the hotel room, where Kadeem was on the bed butt naked and passed out. I sat down in the chair across the bed and pulled out my taser. I shocked him one good time, shaking him from his drug and liquor induced slumber.

"What the fuck!" Kadeem shot up to his feet on the bed. "Shit! Where am I?"

"Sit down," I said calmly. "You're in a hotel room."

Kadeem frowned and then smirked. "You trying to kidnap me, Micah? It doesn't matter what you do. I'm publishing that fucking book. After all the shit all those holier than thou fuckers put me and my family through, they all deserve it."

"You put that book out and you'll be serving time behind bars for statutory rape."

Panic crossed Kadeem's face. I stood up and pulled the raw video up on my phone. I just had screen shots of when Kadeem was fucking the boy. His eyes bulged. He obviously recognized the coach's son. I figured as much.

"What do you want?" Kadeem asked. "I can't pull the book. I already got an six-figure advance."

"I know. I don't want you to not publish the book," I said. I watched his face turn to confusion. "I want to make some last minute edits. You know, switch this information for that information."

"You want me to take out the shit about your brother?"

I nodded. "I read the book already. Me and my boy hacked into your computer when you were uploading some class notes to your cloud storage. It's a pretty good read. Lots of drama and scandal."

"Aside from not going to jail, what are you going to give me in place of your brother? Having a gay choir director is a tired cliché anyways."

"I'll give you the reverend's son. All you have is first story accounts. I can feed you pictures, videos and an online diary documenting every sexual encounter he's had in the last four years. I'm sure Jabari has messed with other church members you had no idea about."

"You would really give me all of that? I thought you and Jabari were friends."

"Shit changes. Right now, I'm just looking out for my family." I sat up and walked over to Kadeem. I held my hand out and asked, "so, do we have a deal?"

Want More Beast?

To ensure you don't miss any book releases text **"BEAST"** to **313131** to get announcements right on your phone and a free copy of TORN.

Other Titles by BEAST

Champion Breed: Twelve Rounds
Champion Breed II: Fight Night
Champion Breed II: Knocked Out

Torn
Torn 2
Torn 3

Burning Sands: Samson's Struggle
Burning Sands 2: Daemon's Revenge
Burning Sands 3: Samson's Retribution
Burning Sands 4: Daemon's Bloodlust
Burning Sands 5: Samson's Survival

61702538R00090

Made in the USA
Lexington, KY
17 March 2017